DOUGLAS WATT is a historian, poet and novelist. He is the author of *The Price of Scotland: Darien, Union and the Wealth of Nations* (2007), a history of the Darien Disaster and its effect on the Union of the Parliaments, which won the Hume Brown Senior Prize in Scottish History in 2008. He was inspired by his extensive investigations into seventeenth century Scotland to create the character of John MacKenzie, loosely based on a real historical figure, and to bring the history of the period to life. He lives in Linlithgow with his wife Julie and their three children. *Death of a Chief* is his first novel.

Praise for *The Price of Scotland* by Douglas Watt:

Many books have been written about the Darien Scheme... but The Price of Scotland *surpasses them all.*
LONDON REVIEW OF BOOKS

...an economist's eye and a poet's sensibility...
THE OBSERVER

Exceptionally well-written... if you're not Scottish and live here – read it. If you're Scottish read it anyway. It's a very, very good book.
I-ON MAGAZINE

...compelling and i
THE SCOTSMAN

By the same author:

History
The Price of Scotland: Darien, Union and the Wealth of Nations
(2007)

Poetry
A History of Moments (2005)

Death of a Chief

DOUGLAS WATT

Luath Press Limited

EDINBURGH

www.luath.co.uk

First published 2009
Reprinted 2009
This edition 2010

ISBN: 978-1-906817-31-2

The author's right to be identified as author of this book
under the Copyright, Designs and Patents Act 1988 has been
asserted.

The publisher acknowledges the support of
 Scottish
Arts Council

towards the publication of this volume.

The paper used in this book is neutral sized and recyclable.
It is made from elemental chlorine free pulps sourced from
renewable forests.

Printed in the UK by CPI Bookmarque, Croydon CRO 4TD

Typeset in 9.7 point Sabon

To Julie

Trust flattering life no more, redeem time past
And live each day as if it were thy last.
William Drummond of Hawthornden (1585–1649)

Acknowledgements

I would like to thank my wife Julie for her love and support. We first dreamed up the story of John MacKenzie and Davie Scougall many years ago. She has been a constant help during the writing of this book, providing a wealth of ideas and improvements. Many thanks to everyone at Luath and to Jennie Renton for her editorial work. I would also like to thank historians Dr Louise Yeoman and Dr John Finlay for answering questions about their specialties in late seventeenth century Scotland. The vision of that time presented in these pages is entirely my own.

PRELUDE
The Battlefield of Inverkeithing

SIR LACHLAN'S EYES rose from the coarsely carved skull on the gravestone to the grey firth, and then to the black outline of the city on the horizon. It was over thirty years since he last stood on this hillside; over thirty years since he stood dripping with the blood of other men. Memories of the carnage flashed through his mind – a slaughter beyond all comprehension. On that day he had witnessed the annihilation of his clan and the death of his chief. As always the images coalesced into the cleaved head of his 14-year-old brother. Sir Lachlan had lost two other brothers that day, but it was always Ruaridh he remembered – taken before his time. The memory was agonising despite the passage of so many years.

His thoughts returned to the night before the battle in 1651. The memories of those hours were less painful. For Sir Lachlan they remained a time of great significance: the last moments with his brothers; the end of his youth; the beginning of a dreary labyrinth of survival.

He remembered resting on the ground, surrounded by his clan. They had travelled all day and the army, a motley host of different kindreds, sprawled over the fields above the small burgh of Inverkeithing. The MacLeans ate a light meal, drank some whisky and listened to their bards recite poems: long, elegiac panegyrics about their chief and his ancestors, vivid descriptions of past battles and incitements to fight bravely in the one to come, which would secure the kingdom for King Charles and bestow honour on the MacLeans of Duart. The haunting words still held their place in Sir Lachlan's memory. Visions of that night came back to him as he stared across the waters of the firth: the scarred face of the old bard; his brothers calmly talking to each other; and then the long silent wait until dawn. Hours later MacLean of Duart and hundreds of his clansmen lay dead on the hillside above the town, their bodies hacked to pieces by Cromwell's army. Sir Lachlan had fought hard, slashing limbs, cleaving bodies – killing, killing, killing.

The emotions of the night before returned: fear that had gripped his stomach like a vice, but also a strange sense of belonging and an intense joy which had made life for those few hours before the battle seem soaked in meaning. Nothing since had come close to those sleepless hours in the pitch-black Fife night.

He was lost in his memories until the cry of a sea bird pulled him back to the present and his eyes focused again on the outline of the city across the firth; a panorama punctuated by high tenements and kirk spires. His heart sank as he remembered the reason for his journey. Edinburgh was a bleak city of lawyers. It represented all that was wrong with his life. He hated the place and the long journeys there from the Highlands. He despised the self-righteous advocates, the dour merchants, the hypocritical ministers in their cold churches and the foul reek of the streets. How different it had been in his youth, the days of action when he had fought for his king against the regicidal monster Cromwell.

He made his way down from the small graveyard on the hill to join the party waiting for him beside their horses. He was a tall man of around sixty years with a worn, weathered face and a periwig on his head, dressed in black cloak and breeches, a basket sword swinging from his belt. As he climbed onto his horse it was plain that he retained some of the strength of his youth that had made him such a ruthless swordsman. The other three men also mounted their horses and followed Sir Lachlan down the mud track towards the burgh of Inverkeithing.

Two of them – hair blowing in the wind, dark complexions, dressed in tartan plaids – barked at each other in Gaelic. The third, a slimmer version of Sir Lachlan, was, like him, dressed in black and wearing a periwig.

CHAPTER I
The Apothecary's Shop

THE APOTHECARY SAT on a tall stool with his back to the door of the shop. He carefully measured a small quantity of liquid in a phial and poured it into a large stone mortar lying before him on a wooden bench at the back wall. Above the bench were shelves lined with bottles of different shapes and sizes, whose multicoloured contents reflected the light from the two candles which lit the room, casting a rainbow over the old man's hands.

As he lifted his head he was just able to determine the names scrawled on the labels of the bottles, flasks, glasses and boxes: *castoreum*, *antimonium*, Peruvian bark, *stribrum*, orange peel, opium, almond oil, *helleboris albus*, *elaterium*, mercury sublimate, arsenic.

His swollen hands reached up to the second shelf and removed a bottle labelled *vitriolum romanum*. He poured a small amount into the mortar and began to grind slowly. He had repeated this procedure on countless occasions – the sound of the pestle on the mortar had accompanied his adult life and he found the process reassuring.

Easing himself slowly off his stool, he made his way painfully to the shelves where he stored an assortment of books and ledgers. He screwed up his eyes as he read the spines. A number of years had passed since he had last made this concoction and it took a while before he found what he was looking for. He removed a dusty tome and returned with it to the bench. Having consulted one of the recipes, he continued his preparation, grinding the mixture down and inhaling the pungent odour deeply until he judged it just right. As he did so, a knock on the door startled him. He turned his head and screwed up his eyes again, trying to make out who it was through the small glass panes in the door. He would be closing in a few minutes – he shut his shop at five and few customers called at this late hour. But he could not make out who the dark figure was behind the door. Forced to leave his stool again, he moved slowly across to the front of the shop until the person could be identified through the thick glass.

He took a long key from his belt and opened the door, which he usually kept locked – he had in store many valuable ingredients and these were dangerous times – although not as bad as some; 1648 had been the worst – plague, war; the death of his wife and two children. He recalled the appalling stench of putrescent buboes. Isabel Leitch from his village, strangled and burned at the stake for witchcraft on the Castle Hill – the poor misguided creature.

The stranger wore a hooded cloak which obscured the face almost to the bottom of the nose. He entered the shop quickly from the vennel outside.

'How can I help you?' asked the apothecary.

CHAPTER 2

A Body is Discovered

THE BODY LAY on a four poster bed. The large head was twisted back, eyes shut. A bloated blue tongue protruded from the mouth. The unnatural position of the arms and legs suggested that the last moments of life had not been peaceful. The man was wearing black breeches and a white linen shirt with a long, yellow stain on the chest. A green and blue tartan plaid lay on the bed beside him.

Nothing moved in the room.

As the sun rose, light entered through a gap at the window where an awning had fallen forward.

The whitewashed bedchamber was furnished in simple fashion: the largest piece of furniture was the bed and there were a couple of cupboards, which were closed. Its beamed ceiling depicted hunting scenes of deer and wolves.

Against one wall was a long table on which rested a few books, a pile of documents, a bottle of wine and one glass. Another solitary book lay on the small cabinet beside the bed.

There was silence in the house of John Smith until the Tron Kirk bell sounded seven times and one of Sir Lachlan's servants, who had spent the night asleep in a small adjoining room, entered his master's bedchamber to wake him with the usual words of Gaelic. As he opened the door, his old eyes could not take in the scene before him. He stood, stupefied, staring at the body of the man he had served faithfully for over forty years. Finally he turned, eyes full of tears, and left to wake his new master, Hector, with the news of the chief's death.

CHAPTER 3
Bad News for John MacKenzie

JOHN MACKENZIE HAD slept later than usual after the previous evening's entertainment. On waking he was annoyed with himself for drinking so much wine and losing five pounds to Sir Lachlan. Then he remembered the songs that had closed the night's celebrations and felt more content. He always found that after a few glasses of claret, his tongue and soul loosened; he was able to shed the constraints of legal life and could speak unrestrainedly in his first language, Gaelic. Tales and jokes seemed to slip into his mind more easily in his native tongue and it was always more amusing when a few Lowlanders who were completely ignorant of the language were in the company. They had certainly teased Davie Scougall and Mr Primrose, and even Mr Hope, who claimed to understand Gaelic because of a family connection on his mother's side – but not the Gaelic spoken after a bottle or two of good wine!

MacKenzie, who was a tall man in his fifties, dressed quickly. He ate his breakfast and was on the point of leaving for the Session when a messenger arrived. He stared down at the short note written by Hector MacLean and the colour drained from his face. 'Good God! I was with Sir Lachlan last night! Do you know what has happened?' he asked the young boy who had delivered it.

'Folk are sayin he killed himsel, sir,' the boy replied.

MacKenzie handed him a coin and closed the door. Then, like a blind man, he staggered through to the bedchamber, reached the window and threw it open so that he might hear the bustle of life from the city beneath. The familiar feeling of nausea rose within him like a wave of pain – then the awful dread – as if something very bad was about to happen – something he knew about but could not quite remember.

Suddenly he bent over and retched on the floor. It was not the news that had overwhelmed him, but the memory of another death. The events of over twenty years ago came rushing back, as they had on countless occasions. The cry of his newborn daughter was as real and close as the sounds from the street; the forlorn face of the midwife, the words 'I'm sorry, John.' Then the grief – terrible grief, and guilt too – guilt that made him want to rip open his chest, pull out his heart and cast it onto a fire.

CHAPTER 4
The Crown Officer

ARCHIBALD STIRLING AND Adam Lawtie arrived at Sir Lachlan's lodgings to find the house in a state of shock. In the living chamber they met Sir Lachlan's son and daughter. Hector's face was pale, his eyes slightly bloodshot. Ann MacLean, more composed, shook hands with the two men and politely accepted their condolences, then returned to a chair at the window, where she sat, motionless, staring down at the High Street. Hector showed them to his father's bedchamber, where they were left to make an examination of the body.

Lawtie spent some minutes poking and prodding the huge corpse. Focusing particular attention on the state of the engorged tongue, he removed a thin metal instrument from his leather bag.

Stirling stood near the door, unable to look at the physician. Lawtie was bent over the corpse, his hunched shoulders presenting an unattractive vision to the Crown Officer, but a preferable one to the image of death that lay sprawled on the bed. Lawtie turned his head towards Stirling, his brow wrinkled.

'Poison, Mr Stirling!'

Stirling rubbed his forehead with his fingers and sighed deeply. He was a fleshy man but had the height to carry his weight without being seen as fat. He had hoped for a natural death so that he might complete a brief report and return home expeditiously.

'What brings you to that conclusion, Mr Lawtie?' he asked, without looking up, his tone betraying that he was annoyed at the physician's conclusion.

'Poison, beyond doubt, sir. The state of the tongue, the position of the limbs, the evident suddenness of the death, all point towards poison.'

Stirling sighed again, this time deeper and longer, as he reflected that he might have to work all day. A detailed report would be required for the Lord Advocate. For some unexplained reason he had been asked to intervene at a very early stage in the investigations. Usually the kin of the deceased would have led the enquiries. Something was afoot – he could be sure of that – and the Advocate wanted him out of the way. It was a most disagreeable prospect. He had planned to work on Gordon of Ruthven's account of the battle of Kilsyth; to recreate in his mind how Montrose had deployed his five thousand foot and six hundred horse.

'Mr Lawtie,' he said, after a few moments reflection, 'would you please prepare an account of your findings and present it to my office tomorrow morning.'

Lawtie nodded, pleased with the prospect of an easy pound or two. He returned his instruments to his small leather bag and left the room.

Stirling forced himself to walk over to the corpse. He had met the deceased many years before when acting as his advocate in a minor case before the Session and had thought him arrogant. He recalled that he had never received any payment. Although the details of the case escaped him, he knew that Sir Lachlan had fought at Inverkeithing on 20 July 1651 – Montrose was dead by then.

He looked at the body of the deceased for a short while;

then round the rest of the room, trying to absorb as much detail as he could for his report.

On entering the living chamber, Stirling caught Hector MacLean's eye and beckoned him over.

'It seems your father has been poisoned, sir.'

Hector's lips trembled slightly. 'Then it is murder, Mr Stirling?'

'Murder... or suicide.'

Hector gazed through the open door that led into Sir Lachlan's chamber. There were tears in his eyes.

'We must begin our investigation, sir,' said Stirling. 'I know this is very difficult for you, but I have to prepare a report for the Advocate. I need to talk with everyone within these lodgings. No one is to leave until I have given my permission. Now, tell me, who is in the house?'

'Only my sister, our landlord John Smith, his wife and child, his servant and my father's... my two men,' replied Hector.

'I must speak to everyone alone. You will arrange this for me and then I must talk with you, sir.' A vision of Montrose came to the Crown Officer – black armour, tight white collar, dark hair down to his shoulders, faint moustache, fine nose – a perfect face... the great Marquis, hung at the Cross of Edinburgh. Stirling recalled the words of a poem Montrose had written during his imprisonment: 'Open all my veins, that I may swim to Thee my saviour, in that crimson lake.' To die with dignity and without fear... to sacrifice oneself for a cause... these were the ideas that inflamed his private passions. He had always been looking for someone to follow. But how could any living man compare with Montrose?

Stirling brought himself back to the present and sat opposite Hector MacLean at the circular oak table in Sir Lachlan's living quarters. The fire burning in the grate cast shadows onto the decorated ceiling beams, bringing to life brightly painted scenes from antiquity and the Bible. A long oak cabinet, with a large candlestick and candle at each end, was the only other piece of furniture in the room. A number of oil paintings portraying Scottish monarchs hung from the walls.

Stirling dipped his quill into a small container of ink and began to write. As he posed his questions, he did not raise his head to look into the eyes of the young chief, who was in his early twenties, but listened attentively and made notes as Hector spoke, his long thin hands gliding across the parchment that lay in front of him.

'At what hour did you last see your father?'

'It must have been after midnight, but before one o'clock, for I heard the bells strike twelve. My father retired to his chamber after our small celebration had ended. He was in unusually good humour following our victory in the Session and had drunk a good deal. We played cards after dining.'

'Who was in attendance here last night?'

'Myself, my father, John Smith, our lawyers – that is, the clerk of the Session Mr John MacKenzie and advocate Mr Francis Primrose – the minister Mr John Hope and Robert Campbell of Glenbeg. We were served by Smith's servant girl and our two men remained in the room throughout the evening. I presume that Smith's wife and child were also in the house. And of course, I almost forgot, David Scougall, MacKenzie's new writer, was also present. He did not play cards and barely touched a drop of wine all evening.'

'And where was your sister, sir?'

Hector cleared his throat.

'Ann was visiting one of her close friends – the daughter of Sir William Dunbar. She often spends the night at Drumliston House when we are in Edinburgh. My father and Dunbar were in exile together.'

'Why had your father come to Edinburgh?'

'As I have already mentioned, Mr Stirling, we had a case before the Session against Menzies of Pitcairn in order to determine title over lands. There has been a long-standing dispute about the rights to Ardintrive. Menzies claimed that since he had tenants *in situ,* possession was his. We based our claim on a purchase made in 1573 by my ancestor and namesake Hector MacLean of Glenshieldaig. My father wished to wadset the land to raise cash. Mr MacKenzie and Mr Primrose will be able to give you a more detailed account of the legal proceedings over the years and their tortuous history.'

'Did your father have any contact with Menzies after the case was heard in the Session?'

'I did not see him do so, nor did he refer to it.'

Stirling fell silent for a few moments and his thoughts gravitated, as they often did, to the execution of Montrose – his beauty defiled by the Covenanters, the gruesome quartering of his body, his head stuck on a spike at the Tolbooth – such butchery in the name of God. He coughed and forced his mind back to the matter in hand.

'It was common knowledge that your father was not, how shall I put it, sir, a man of happy disposition – he was deep in debt and many creditors were at law against him. Is it possible that he ended his own life?'

Hector inhaled deeply.

'I do not believe so. He was indeed troubled by financial misfortune, but my father was not the kind of man to run away from a fight. He thrived upon legal disputation.'

'Can you think of anyone who might want to kill your father, or who might have benefited from his death?'

'It's true that my father has made many enemies through the years and debt has been his undoing. The lands of Glenshieldaig were devastated during the Great Rebellion. Rents collapsed to practically nothing. The huge debts accumulated by the family in the early part of the century could not be serviced. Despite attempts by my father to reduce the burden of debt by boosting the income of his lands from the cattle trade, the total continued to swell, like a tumour on the House. Many of his creditors have not been repaid. I regret this very much, for it leaves our family on a weak footing.'

'Was Menzies of Pitcairn such an enemy?'

'The case still stands in law and so he would have gained nothing. I think it very unlikely.'

'Were you and your father on good terms?'

Hector slowly drew the fingers of his right hand into a fist. For some reason the small pamphlet which his father had penned for him when he came of age appeared in his mind. *Advice to My Son*, intended to provide him with some pointers in life, was full of pithy nuggets such as: 'I can recommend no more useful and dignified recreation than the golf'; 'Spend time at Court – a man with no interest at Court is like a bee without a sting'; 'Refrain from gambling, drinking and lechery.' If only his father had followed his own maxims.

The young chief opened his hand again.

'We had our differences. What father and son do not? My father was a man of strong opinions, a great man for tradition, for wine, the table and trips to Court in London. He was not well disposed towards change or towards my suggestions for increasing the produce of his land so that debts might be redeemed. He opposed cutting the cost of the household at Glenshieldaig and stood firm against the policies being pursued by many other chiefs, some of them our neighbours, who have increased rents.'

'Can you provide me with an inventory of his debts? That might prove useful.'

'I will see that one of our lawyers attends to it.'

Stirling rested his quill for a moment and threw a piercing look at Hector.

'Robert Campbell of Glenbeg. Why did Sir Lachlan keep such company?'

'Glenbeg has always been close to my father.'

'Is that not most unusual, sir, for your father to be on such friendly terms with a Campbell laird?'

'True, my father did not count many Campbells amongst his friends. The MacLeans have a profound loathing for the Clan Campbell and Highland feuds burn deep. But Glenbeg was a strange fish. He had fought against his own clan in the Wars of the Covenant; he'd been with my father at the Battle of Inverkeithing and spent many years in exile with him. He too is prone to melancholia and has sought oblivion in drink and the table, although I believe Glenbeg pursued his vices much deeper than my father. His debts became insurmountable and he was forced to relinquish his own lands to a commission of clansmen and neighbours. I was surprised to see him here last night, for I knew he could not afford to make further losses at the table. But the love of cards is a disease from which men are not easily cured.'

'Thank you, sir,' said Stirling, noting the expression in the tired eyes of the young chief. 'That will be all for now. Please find your sister and tell her that I wish to talk with her.'

Ann MacLean entered the chamber and sat at the table. Stirling could see that she had been crying and at once felt sympathy for her. Ann's beauty did not escape him. She wore a simple dark gown which drew the eye to her graceful white neck. Her hair was tied back and there was a black gauze pinner upon her head.

'My lady,' he began, 'I will not detain you long, but the

nature of your father's death makes it necessary.'

Ann MacLean's face paled. 'My father was a difficult man but I loved him,' she said.

'I am sorry that I must ask you this. Can you think of any reason why your father would take his own life?'

'Never! He would never have destroyed himself!'

There was silence for a few moments, broken at last by the Tron Kirk bell. Stirling waited until it had sounded ten times.

'Can you tell me where you were last night?'

'I went to the house of my friend, Isabella Dunbar, the daughter of Sir William Dunbar. I arrived in the late afternoon, after spending some time here watching Henryson paint my father's portrait. Isabella and I had our supper when it got dark, and then we played on the virginal. After some conversation we retired to our bedchamber.'

'Was it common for you to remain overnight at the house of Sir William?'

'Yes – I have no time for dull evenings with my father's friends. I find the company of his lawmen tiresome and his soirées always finish with ridiculous poems and tales of battles, and then Gregor McIan is ordered to take out his fiddle.'

'You are not a speaker of the Gaelic tongue?'

'It is my first language but it belongs to the past, Mr Stirling – a past of clan battles and of bitter poetry celebrating slaughter. I choose not to speak it. English is the tongue of the future,' she said defiantly.

'You did, I trust, leave on good terms with your father yesterday afternoon?'

'As good as ever. My father and I had our disagreements, especially about my marriage. He wanted me to have a local laird as a husband for the good of our kindred and the future standing of the House of Glenshieldaig. Mr Stirling, when I was growing up I spent much time at Court in London. My father made many journeys there in the vain hope of receiving favours from the late King Charles and his father for loyal service during the Great Rebellion. Have you ever tasted the life of London? If so, you might understand why I find this cold city not to my liking. The damp castles of the Highlands hold even less appeal. My father felt I was being disloyal. My mother had to intervene between us many times.'

'And you will now marry whom you please?'

'That will depend on my brother.'

'I must ask, my lady – have you noticed anything that might shed some light upon the sudden death of your father?'

'Nothing.'

Stirling lapsed into thought for a few moments. Montrose's mother Margaret Ruthven died when he was in his sixth year. He had perhaps not thought deeply enough about her influence on him.

'Has Lady MacLean been informed of this terrible event?'

'Yes, word has already been sent north.'

'If I may ask but one further question. How were relations between your mother and father?'

'As you might expect there were disagreements but they have been together for almost thirty years and have great fondness for each other. I fear my mother will be devastated.'

'Will you see her soon?'

'I will travel north with our kinsmen when they come for my father's body.'

'Those are all my questions for now.'

Stirling allowed his eyes to drift up to the painted ceiling, which was of a most impressive standard. He must ask John Smith who was responsible for it – his own chamber would certainly benefit from the attention of such an artist.

His gaze rested on a voluptuous female figure in a scene from antiquity. His wife would certainly appreciate their chamber ceiling being painted in such a manner – and he would be rewarded in the way he liked. But this dreadful affair had to be concluded first.

CHAPTER 5
Memories of the Night Before

MACKENZIE PUT HIS head out of the window into the cold morning air and took long, deep breaths. The powerful memories began to fade and with them the sickness and sense of panic. All that remained was the residue of sadness, which he knew would always be there. He could not shake off the sense that he was being punished for his sins, despite his own rational arguments.

As he sat down in a chair, a vision of Sir Lachlan came back to him – his large head swaying, cheeks bright red, singing a beautiful Gaelic song about a young woman lamenting the death of her husband. Everyone present had been moved, even the Lowlanders. MacKenzie had been especially touched, for his wife had often sung this song when they sat together in the evening.

A knock on the door interrupted his thoughts. Davie Scougall stood before him.

'Have you heard the news sir? Sir Lachlan MacLean is dead!' Scougall announced, in considerable agitation.

'Indeed, Davie, I have. I was just on the point of departing for his lodgings. Come, let us walk there together.'

The two men made their way down the winding stone stairs. Scougall was considerably shorter than MacKenzie, by perhaps a foot. There was a darkness round his mouth and on his cheeks and neck, suggesting a razor had to be applied twice a day to contain the growth of his facial hair. They emerged onto the bustling High Street. Stone tenements, some up to six storeys in height, enclosed the wide road on both sides. The fine weather of the early morning had given way to dark clouds and as they walked downhill in the direction of the Canongate it began to drizzle.

On reaching Smith's house, they were shown into the room where only a few hours before they had dined with Sir Lachlan. They spoke briefly with Hector MacLean before being presented to the Crown Officer.

'Ah, John!' said Stirling, 'I am glad you are here. My Lord Advocate sets me to it with great haste – it appears the case is of some importance to him – or perhaps he wants me out of the office at this difficult time. He suffers much from what he calls "politics". Anyway, maybe you can shed some light on this grim affair.'

'Archibald, let me introduce my young friend Davie Scougall,' said MacKenzie. 'Davie, Archibald and I were students together at Aberdeen.'

Stirling and Scougall shook hands.

MacKenzie continued, 'This is indeed a dark hour. How did my old friend meet his end?'

'It seems he died by poison, administered either by his own hand or through the agency of another. At least, that is the view of our learned medical friend Mr Lawtie, whose report should be presented to my office tomorrow. I have already spoken with most of those who were present last night: Hector MacLean, John Smith, his wife, his servant girl and also to Ann MacLean, who was visiting a friend. I now await Mr Hope, Mr Primrose and the Laird of Glenbeg. If you both care to sit down I would like to ask some questions.'

MacKenzie and Scougall seated themselves at the oak table.

'John, would you please give me a full account of the events of last night and whether you noticed anything pertinent to Sir Lachlan's death?'

'Davie and I arrived at about eight o'clock. Mr Hope was already here, administering one of his famous cold remedies to Sir Lachlan, who had complained of suffering from such a condition when we met in the Periwig Inn the previous evening. Perhaps ten minutes later Mr Primrose arrived, and then Campbell of Glenbeg, a few minutes after that. We ate a fine meal – roast mutton in blood, ragout of rabbits, pottage, roast pigeons, finished off with tarts and boiled pudding, if I remember correctly. We also drank freely from John Smith's wine cellar. At around ten we began our cards which we played for perhaps two hours. Songs and poetry, mostly in Gaelic, ended the evening's entertainment. Davie and I left at about thirty minutes after midnight accompanied by Mr Primrose and Mr Hope. I do not know when Glenbeg departed. During the evening we all left the room on a number of occasions to pass water. Smith's servant girl moved in and out with food and drink. Sir Lachlan's two men were in the room throughout. I noticed nothing out of the ordinary, although I must confess that the claret jug may have blunted my powers of observation. Perhaps Davie might provide you with a clearer picture of the later part of the evening.'

'Does Mr MacKenzie's description concur with what you can remember, Mr Scougall?' asked Stirling.

'Yes, sir,' replied Scougall, his mind racing back through the previous evening. An image appeared to him, he hesitated and an incomprehensible sound came from his mouth. He was forced to continue to save himself further embarrassment: 'There was one thing – it may be nothing. I did think it somewhat odd. I would not want to suggest something that did not exist. During the songs at the end of the evening, Smith's

servant girl spoke privately to Mr Hope. I was... disturbed by
the look that enveloped his face. I fear the spirit of lust had
been awakened in him – and he briefly placed his hand upon
her. But as Mr MacKenzie has said, we departed with him and
he came up the High Street with us as far as the Tron Kirk.'

Scougall was interrupted by the arrival of one of Sir
Lachlan's men. On being informed that Primrose and Hope
had arrived, Stirling said, 'John, I would be obliged if you
could meet me at my chambers in the Session tonight so that I
may share my findings with you and benefit from some of your
wise counsel. I believe that you know the characters involved
better than I.'

'Of course, Archibald. But before I leave, may I view Sir
Lachlan's chamber?'

'I must come with you to ensure that nothing is
disturbed.'

As they approached the door, Stirling took hold of the cuff
of MacKenzie's jacket and lowered his voice so that no one
else could hear.

'Do you think that Sir Lachlan would take his own life?'

'I've been his legal agent for over twenty years and I do not
believe that his nature made him capable of self-destruction.'

They entered the chief's chambers, Scougall following
reluctantly behind. The corpse had been attended to, the limbs
straightened and the body covered with a sheet of white linen.
MacKenzie walked over to it and pulled the sheet back to reveal
Sir Lachlan's large, wigless head. His eyes were closed and he
looked at peace. Noticing the bilious stain on his white shirt,
the advocate replaced the sheet and walked slowly round the
chamber, his eyes seeming to devour the objects in the room.
Scougall stood at the door, transfixed by the shape underneath
the white cloth.

'Until tonight, Archibald,' said MacKenzie, his perusal of

the scene complete. He kept his own counsel as he and Scougall made their way back up the High Street.

'I must return to my house early in the morning, Davie,' he said, as they reached the Tron Kirk. 'Why not travel out tomorrow yourself? My man will bring you a map. It will give us a chance to probe the potential causes of this tragedy. My daughter will have a meal prepared and you can spend the night, then we will travel back to Edinburgh together the following day.'

'I would be most honoured, sir.'

MacKenzie bowed his head, smiled and strode off in the direction of the Court of Session. Within moments, he had disappeared into the busy thoroughfare.

CHAPTER 6
Scougall Takes the Country Air

DAVIE SCOUGALL HIRED a horse from the landlord of the Targe Tavern. Having tentatively accustomed himself to the feel of the beast, for he was a reluctant and uneasy horseman, he rode slowly, through the West Port and out into the open fields that surrounded Edinburgh. He followed the track along the Water of Leith, a small river which wound its way through the Lothian countryside to find the sea at the Port of Leith. The fine weather and the clear blue sky made the journey agreeable. He began to relax and shed the stiff skin he wore in the city.

As his horse climbed the hill above the village of Colinton, he passed two young women who looked up and smiled at him. Thus far in life Scougall had very little experience of the female sex. His energies had been focused on learning the art of the notary public, religious reflection and golf. But something about one of the girl's smiles and the curve of her figure made the idea of taking her in his arms most appealing. He decided that it was time he devoted some of his energy towards marriage, recalling Ecclesiastes, Chapter 9: 'Live joyfully with the wife whom thou lovest all the days of the life of thy vanity, which he hath given thee under the sun.'

Scougall lost himself in reflections on the female sex and it was only when his old horse plodded into Currie, a village comprising a few small cottages, that he was stirred from these pleasantly sinful thoughts and remembered why he was making his way towards the Pentland Hills, for Currie was the last village MacKenzie had drawn on the map that had been delivered to him the night before.

Scougall respected MacKenzie's abilities as an advocate and clerk of the Session and had always found him to be a most affable and good humoured man who had treated him with the utmost courtesy. However, there were aspects of his character that were disturbing. He obviously had little sympathy for the brethren of the Covenant and at times could slip into mockery. Scougall decided to ask him to explain his religious views more clearly so that he could set his own mind at rest. And he found it hard to thole MacKenzie's propensity to speak in Gaelic – the language of Godless barbarians! Scougall rebuked himself for thinking in this way about a man who had offered him nothing but kindness and who was soon to entertain him in his own dwelling place. Yes, MacKenzie was a most skilled lawyer, he told himself, of that there could be no doubt because of his large number of clients. Mostly from the Highlands, he could not help observing, then reminded himself that they included some from good Lowland stock, and a few at least were Presbyterians. Scougall thought himself fortunate to have been recommended by Hugh Dallas, under whom he had served his apprenticeship. He intended to make the most of the path providence had provided for him and chided himself for having thought so disrespectfully of such an honourable man.

The track eventually came to a small stone brig which led back across the Water of Leith. Scougall stopped his horse to appreciate the panorama opening up before him – a series of undulating fields and in the distance the dark green and brown of the Pentland Hills, the 'Highlands of the Lothians', as MacKenzie was fond of calling them. To his left, on the other side of the river, was a wood of birk, oak and fir, and through the trees, a house was visible now and again as the branches moved in the breeze. Scougall crossed the bridge and proceeded down a path which opened into a white avenue of hawthorns.

At the end was a tall wooden gate set in a high stone wall which appeared to encircle the house. He climbed down from his horse and pushed the gate open, then stopped in his tracks, truly astounded by what he saw. He had not imagined MacKenzie would inhabit a dwelling place which far outshone the so-called 'Palace' of Sir George Bruce that he had once visited in Culross.

The house was three storeys high, harled in bright white with crow gables and a red pantiled roof. The plain style of the vernacular architecture was offset by a delightful garden. To his left were shrubs and trees. To his right was a huge lawn bordered by flower beds, in the centre of which were four yew trees planted together, each perhaps twenty feet in height. In front of the house was a carved fountain from which water soporifically gurgled. Scougall felt as if he had stumbled upon the Garden of Eden: 'And the Lord God planted a garden eastward in Eden; and there he put the man whom he had formed. And out of the ground made the Lord God to grow every tree that is pleasant to the sight, and good for food; the tree of life also in the midst of the garden, and the tree of knowledge of good and evil.' He noticed a man standing at the door of the house and realised it was MacKenzie.

'Welcome, Davie! I trust your journey has not been too arduous.'

MacKenzie's servant took the reins of Scougall's horse and led it to the stables behind the house.

'Such a majestic house!' Scougall gabbled. 'And what gardens! There can be none finer in the whole kingdom.'

'Then you have not seen many of the gardens in this kingdom, Davie,' laughed MacKenzie. 'Scotland has many fine gardens. Look no further than Eskdale House, a few miles from your own Musselburgh. There you will find a much larger and more splendid park. Indeed, in the years of peace since the Restoration many of our landed men have spent much of their precious time, and even more of their precious money, on horticulture. I must organise a tour of the gardens of the Lothians for you. The art of gardening is a most beneficial occupation for professional men like us. This garden has taken over twenty years to nurture into its present shape. I will take you on the Grand Tour later, but first you must meet my daughter.'

MacKenzie led Scougall through the doorway into the house. As he passed under the lintel, the young notary noticed an inscription. It appeared to be in a language which was not Latin, and did not seem to be French.

'What tongue is this, sir?' he asked.

'Gaelic, Davie.'

'And what does it say?'

'*Chan fhiach taigh mòr gun straighlich*,' said MacKenzie, and then translated: 'A great house without noise is worth nothing.'

Scougall looked baffled.

'Now, Davie, here she is.'

A young woman in her early twenties dressed in a plain linen gown with a laced shift and apron entered the hall. She was not as striking as Ann MacLean but she had an attractive face and warm smile. Scougall could not help admiring her figure.

'Elizabeth, this is Mr Scougall,' said MacKenzie, 'Davie, my daughter.'

For a few moments Scougall was lost for words as he gazed

at the auburn hair tied loosely at her neck, falling in ringlets at the back. The dark eyes flashed like her father's. Elizabeth smiled up at the young clerk, for she was not tall, and Scougall murmured a greeting.

'I am sure that you must be hungry after your journey, Mr Scougall. Dinner will be ready in a short while. Perhaps, father, you might offer our guest a glass of wine in the library.'

'An excellent idea, Beth.'

Scougall followed MacKenzie into a room full of books. Two large windows looked out onto a small lawn with a stone sundial at its centre. Behind were shrubs and trees and then the high sandstone wall that enclosed the garden. Scougall's eyes wandered round the room. On one wall was a large richly carved, wooden fireplace; on the others, bookcases reached from floor to ceiling.

MacKenzie beckoned him to peruse his library. There were works in Latin and Greek, English and Scots, and European languages. In the English section he spotted the names of Alexander, Donne, Drayton, Douglas, King James I, Jonson, Shakespeare – writers he had heard of but not read; in French were Bèze, Bodin, Chassanion, Du Moulin, Marot, Montaigne, Rabelais; in Italian, Ariosto, Boccaccio, Groto, Machiavelli, Ochino, Tasso; in the classical section Aristotle, Cicero, Plato, Ramus and many more – Bibles, commentaries, legal texts, philosophies, medical books, poetry and theologies. Scougall was overwhelmed by the number and the range of subjects. There were hundreds and hundreds of books. His hand randomly selected one and pulled it out – John Napier of Merchiston's *Ouverture de tous les secrets de l'apocalypse ou revelation de S. Iean* published by Brenouzet at La Rochelle in 1602. He quickly replaced it and thought of his own small library of half a dozen texts – he must broaden his reading. His eyes lit on a work of which he himself was the proud owner – Grundy's *The Mask of Prelacy Removed.*

'Are you a follower of Mr Grundy?' inquired Scougall hopefully.

MacKenzie smiled. 'I have read a few of his dull pages! His arguments lost me. I much prefer real philosophers like Aristotle and Plato. Such men can tell us a thing or two about the nature of things.'

'I fear they were heathens, sir,' said Scougall seriously.

'Here, there are studies of human nature made through the ages,' MacKenzie continued, unperturbed. 'And it is through understanding human nature that we will determine who was responsible for Sir Lachlan's death. I believe that the old chief did not take his life.'

'How can you be sure, sir?' Scougall was struck by the certitude of MacKenzie's manner.

'Each individual who was present in John Smith's house on the night of the murder, as well as Sir Lachlan's daughter who was not, has provided an account of events. Combining such evidence with a study of the characters and applying the principles of rational philosophy will enable us to come to an understanding of what happened. The identity of the person, or persons, responsible for this atrocious murder will be revealed. I have always been disturbed and fascinated by my fellow man, the study of whom is infinitely more fruitful than any attempt to probe the nature of God. I regret to say that the more I read of religion's mysterious texts and tortuous treaties on church government, the less I understand; while as I delve deeper into the study of man, the more I am amazed by his complexities.' He smiled at his young friend who was finding it a challenge to arrange his features in the requisite contours of respect and intelligent appreciation. MacKenzie ignored his discomfiture, filled two glasses with red wine and handed one to Scougall.

When they entered the dining room, Elizabeth was standing at the table. She had removed her apron and was smoothing down her skirts. Her hair was now tied up and she wore a delicate lace pinner upon her head.

Like the library, the dining room looked out onto the garden. It was decorated with a few oil paintings and some fine pieces of wooden furniture. The table was set for dinner with silver cutlery.

'My father tells me you are most accomplished with a golf club, Mr Scougall,' said Elizabeth with a glint in her eye.

'Yes, indeed,' began Scougall, 'although I do not mean to boast.' He felt his face beginning to flush again. He cursed his fumbling nature.

'You must reveal to me the mysteries of the game. I am a keen follower of the sport and I have even hit a few balls myself.'

'I did not realise that women played.'

'Why, our own Queen Mary was a golfer!'

'But she was a Papist – and an adulteress!'

'What I mean is that women are quite capable of placing a ball on the ground and giving it a blow with a wooden stick,' Elizabeth parried, with no visible reaction to his gauche outburst.

Scougall was on the point of citing a sermon by his local minister on how sport was not a fit pursuit for the weaker sex, when Elizabeth continued, 'Now – tell me the news from town. Have you heard anything more about the death of Sir Lachlan? I am desperate to hear what you know, since you were one of the last people to see him alive.'

Detecting the potential inference that he could be suspected of involvement, Scougall was most indignant: 'I can assure you, Miss MacKenzie, that I had no hand in this affair and I am almost certain your father is also innocent!'

MacKenzie and his daughter laughed.

'You are indeed good company, Davie,' said MacKenzie. 'You amuse me more than any lawyer I know. I have already told you I consider myself to be a keen student of human nature and, having made a close examination of your character since we first met a few weeks ago, I am convinced you are incapable of killing anyone. Now, eat up – you'll not find a more delicate capon in the whole of the Lothians. We also have wild fowl and pigeon pie. I promised to show you my garden. Once we've eaten I suggest we take a walk before it gets dark.'

CHAPTER 7

An Interview in the Garden

OUTSIDE, THE SUN was low in the sky and only birdsong disturbed the silence. As MacKenzie and Scougall sauntered over one of the lawns, the young notary paused occasionally to admire a particular plant in the long herbaceous border on one side. Only a few flowers were visible as specks of colour in the rising green, for it was early spring.

'In the summer my border is glorious,' said MacKenzie. 'I must remember to give you a copy of Reid's *Scots Gard'ner* to take home with you. When you've saved enough money to buy a property, you can plan a garden yourself.'

Under a cluster of trees was a small bench.

'Now, Davie,' MacKenzie observed, as they sat down. 'Is this not a place where men can think in peace?'

'It is too beautiful a spot to ponder death, sir,' replied Scougall.

'Perhaps, but we must put our minds to it. I fear that Mr Stirling has not got to grips with the case. He is a careful and competent lawyer but lacks the motivation that will drive him on to the end. His head is mostly full of history, Davie. For many years, he has been working on a book about the Great Rebellion and that subject has come to dominate his attention. Men who are too concerned with the past often neglect the present. However, I spoke to him at length last night and he showed me notes from his interviews. There is a maze of detail, so I will attempt to pull together what I consider vital strands for you. Tell me – have you formed any opinion as to what actually took place.'

'Sir Lachlan may have taken his own life, but that seems unlikely,' Scougall ventured, adding, 'From our two short meetings, I could see that he was a man of strong opinions who might easily make enemies and he was perhaps not on the best of terms with Hector.'

'Very good, Davie,' MacKenzie nodded. 'I see you are, like me, a keen student of human nature. In his statement to Mr Stirling, Hector admitted he and his father often argued about estate policy. He said that he retired to bed after we had all left, and remembered nothing out of the ordinary. He admits drinking more than was usual. The question is, did he have a motive for killing his father?'

Scougall was still pondering this when MacKenzie continued: 'Sir Lachlan's daughter was at the house of her friend Isabella Dunbar and only returned home in the morning. She was on bad terms with her father because she opposed his desire to marry her to a Highland laird.'

'We cannot blame her for preferring the civilised society of the Lowlands to the barbaric climate of those hills and lochs,' said Scougall, oblivious to any offence he might cause. He was merely reflecting a view of the Highlands shared by many Lowlanders – one that he felt as instinctively as he knew that Louis King of France was an agent of the Antichrist.

MacKenzie smiled at the younger man, whose essential honesty he regarded as a virtue against which lack of tact faded into insignificance. He saw himself as Scougall's mentor. In any case, he had always enjoyed a challenge.

'You have still not made a visit to the Highlands, Davie. I believe you will be surprised with what you find there. Let us, for now, keep our minds on Sir Lachlan's death and lay aside our prejudices,' he said kindly but firmly. 'There is more of interest in the other statements. John Smith attested that he and his wife went to bed immediately after the guests had departed. Woken by a noise, he went out to the staircase and glimpsed a figure turning up onto the next floor. It was too dark to discern much, although he was sure he saw a shoe buckle reflected in the light from his candle. Smith assumed that the man on the stair had been the chief's son, or one of his men. As he got back into bed, the Tron Kirk bell struck twice and he fell asleep. Smith's wife corroborated his assertion that he only left their bedchamber for a matter of minutes. She, too, heard the kirk bell. As far as I am aware, Mr Smith is held in high regard in the burgh, but I do know from my legal work for Sir Lachlan, and here I speak in strict confidence, Davie, that the chief owed Smith a considerable sum of money. Sir Lachlan had failed to pay interest on two bonds and had built up large arrears of boarding expenses.'

Scougall felt deeply flattered that MacKenzie considered him worthy of being made his confidant.

'Is it possible that Smith and his wife murdered Sir Lachlan?' he enquired.

'Possible, but unlikely. Remember, they would not necessarily receive any payments after Sir Lachlan's death. And Smith has many other business ventures that are no doubt more profitable than lending money to a Highland chief. However, his description of a dark figure on the stairs is something that we must keep at the front of our minds. Moving on to Mr Primrose, he, like yourself, noticed Mr Hope flirting with Smith's servant. And of course he left with us. His lodgings are in Borthwick's Wynd. What is your opinion of Mr Primrose?'

'I think he is very ambitious to do well in the law and I am sure he will take his place on that most distinguished bench alongside their Lordships one day. I must admit I feel somewhat daunted in his company even though he is the same age as me.'

'You have painted a very fair picture of him, Davie. He is a gifted young man and aims for the top. There's nothing wrong with that. But I think he sometimes works at it too hard. You should invite him onto the golf course and bring him down a peg or two. Now, where were we? Ah, yes, Mr Hope's account concurred with our testimonies, for he left the lodgings with us. Smith's servant girl shed no further light on the affair. She retired to her chamber on the top floor after the guests had left. Sir Lachlan's two men gave garbled accounts for they both speak little of the Lowland tongue. It seems that after the departure of the guests Sir Lachlan allowed them to finish a bottle or two of wine – deep slumber followed soon after.'

'That only leaves Campbell of Glenbeg.'

'Yes – and it appears that Glenbeg has absconded! He was not found in his miserable lodging in Craig's Wynd when Stirling's man went to fetch him and he was seen by one of the city guards leaving by the West Port in the early morning. Glenbeg is a man on whom good fortune has not shone, Davie. As the fourth son of Duncan Campbell of Glenlochy, he was granted the lands of Glenbeg by his father and spent heavily on building a fine castle on the banks of Loch Beg. But he borrowed too much to fund the construction. Those who lend to such men have much to answer for. His great appetite for wine, the table, and other vices plunged him into a quagmire of debt. Impoverished, he opposed his own clan in the Covenanting Wars. This was the action of a very desperate man, for bonds of kinship in the Highlands have a peculiar power. It is very rare for someone in his position to act against his own clan. He became a friend of Sir Lachlan's during those dark days – they fought together at the bloody slaughter of

Inverkeithing – and he followed him into exile with King Charles. His love of the table was insatiable. *Chluicheadh e h-uile bun rùdain deth*, as we might say in Gaelic – he would play his very knuckles off. He even owed Sir Lachlan money. His melancholic temperament drove him into an abyss of debauchery. It's said that to pay off his debts he sought the intercession of necromancers and sold his soul to the Devil. But the truth is more prosaic: he raised his tenants' rents. Finally he was forced by his own clansmen, many of whom were creditors, to give up his lands. George Campbell, a merchant from Inverary to whom he owed large sums, gained possession of his castle. Since then, Glenbeg has wandered the world begging an existence, friendless except for Sir Lachlan. Perhaps the chief recognised in him a kindred spirit, or saw in him what he himself might have become.'

'But do you really think he killed Sir Lachlan, sir? I know from my own experience that a man who is ruled by the bottle can be dragged very low and commit acts of abomination. My uncle was a respected merchant from Musselburgh who had prospered in the fishing trade. But his ship was wrecked one night in a terrible storm and he lost everything, as he was not insured. This misfortune drove him to drink and he began to violently mistreat my dear aunt. One night, he was seen cursing the sea in a stream of obscenities, when he slipped and fell into the icy water. He must have struck his head on a rock. There was no saving him. His body was recovered the next day. The drink did that to him. Perhaps it has rotted the soul of Glenbeg and driven him to murder the only man who showed him kindness.'

Scougall at once regretted saying quite so much on the subject of his uncle and was relieved when MacKenzie remained focused on the case in hand.

'Tell me, when we were shown the body of Sir Lachlan,

did you notice anything in his chamber?'

'I'm afraid my eyes were transfixed on the corpse. I could take in nothing else.'

'I was much the same. The sight of Sir Lachlan's body was deeply disturbing to me. I had known him for many years and although he was a difficult man, I counted him as a friend. However, I forced myself to examine the chamber, for it was highly likely that little had been disturbed since his death. The first thing to catch my eye was an empty wine glass, lying on its side. It had been knocked over and some red wine spilt onto a book – one of Sir Lachlan's favourites, I believe, a manuscript account of the conquests of Alexander the Great. My eye was then attracted by the papers on the table beside the bed. Legal documents – charters, instruments of sasine and bonds, which bore the appearance of having been examined in haste. They were in a heap which would have made any good notary despair. Some were even lying on the floor. This suggests to me that, after killing Sir Lachlan, the murderer made a hasty search of these documents. I know that the chief was generally careful in the organisation of his papers and so I had a brief look at them. They were all concerned with Sir Lachlan's case before the Session against Menzies of Pitcairn. A full examination of the documents will be required to determine if any are missing. Perhaps you could make an inventory of them tomorrow, Davie?'

MacKenzie, who had been gazing at his garden as he spoke, looked Scougall full in the face.

'You seem puzzled,' he commented.

'I am annoyed with myself, sir. I can remember nothing of the scene, not even the clothing worn by Sir Lachlan. You have recalled so much.'

MacKenzie patted his companion gently on the back.

'We have spoken enough of such matters. The sun is almost

setting and I still have to show you the rest of my garden. Let us take the evening air and talk of other things.'

As the light faded and the sky became imbued with a violet hue, MacKenzie led Scougall once more through his beloved garden, trying to instil into the sceptical young man the mysterious joys of horticulture, telling him the Latin names of particular plants and the difficulty or ease with which he had nurtured them. He stopped beside a patch of dark blue irises and pulled one of the blossoms towards him. 'Here is *Iris germanica*, a native of the Mediterranean region, which has been cultivated longer than any other. An amazing plant. The stems rise at incredible speed in the spring, bursting forth into these tongues of colour.'

Although of the opinion that a love of gardening is only truly inspired in those who have already experienced human love, in a way of which Scougall was ignorant, MacKenzie continued in this vein until they returned to the front door. Scougall had tired of horticulture. His thoughts had drifted from plants to MacKenzie's daughter. He hoped dearly, despite his shyness, that she had not retired to bed.

'We will rise early tomorrow,' said MacKenzie as they entered the house. 'We must be back in Edinburgh before the town is awake. You will accompany me to Mr Hope's manse, which is on our way, and then I will dispatch you to Mr Primrose's lodgings, where an inventory of Sir Lachlan's legal documents is to be found. Primrose will help us draw up a list of the chief's creditors. I intend to pay another visit to Mr Stirling and then if the weather is clement, I suggest we retire to the Links for some recreation. What do you say, Davie?'

Scougall nodded appreciatively at the prospect of an afternoon's golf. MacKenzie's servant, an old man with a long face who said nothing because he spoke little English, showed him to his chamber.

CHAPTER 8
Breakfast at the Manse

MACKENZIE'S MAN SUMMONED Scougall to breakfast with a loud knock on his door. After a hurried meal of bread and ale, the young notary found himself back on his horse, disappointed not to have had the opportunity to say goodbye to Elizabeth, who had retired to bed early the previous evening and had not yet risen.

John Hope's manse was a two-storey dwelling surrounded by an ancient graveyard, was on the outskirts of Edinburgh. The small stone church, a simple rectangular building with a squat, square spire, was a stone's throw from the front door. The two lawyers left their horses at the gates and proceeded along the path which meandered through the gravestones.

'Cemeteries have much to teach us about family history,' said MacKenzie. 'Amongst those buried here is your famous divine Zacharias Grundy. On another occasion we must return and search for his monument.'

MacKenzie continued his discussion of the historical importance of funerary monuments until they reached the manse, then his tone changed. Scougall had not heard him speak with such earnestness before.

'Now, Davie, I must ask you not to be shocked by the manner in which I address Mr Hope. It is only the old lawyer in me. An advocate's questions can seem cruel. It is sometimes necessary to use harsh words to disarm your opponent,' he said, in a voice devoid of its usual conviviality.

A servant showed them into the dining chamber where Mr Hope was enjoying, to Scougall's astonished eyes, a breakfast on the scale of a small feast. In addition to a plate of smoked fish, there were eggs and Scots collops.

The minister indicated that they should join him at the table. After masticating on a particularly large mouthful of fish, he wiped his mouth with a white cloth, smiled and addressed them.

'Now, Mr MacKenzie, Mr Scougall, this is indeed a pleasure, although it is God's will that we meet this morning under a cloud of mourning for our dear departed friend. He was indeed a fine man. Brave, generous…'

MacKenzie cut in, 'Mr Hope. I too regret that our visit is not a social call. You were seen returning to Sir Lachlan's lodgings an hour after departing from us on the High Street. Tell me what you know about Sir Lachlan's death.'

'I know nothing sir… I saw nothing!' said the minister, highly disconcerted.

'I suggest that you close the door, Mr Hope,' the advocate continued, 'lest other ears hear our business.'

The minister paled. He rose, stumbled to the door and quietly shut it. The only sounds in the small chamber were the occasional crackle from the fire and the strained breathing of the corpulent man of God.

'Mr Hope, I suggest you begin with our departure on the High Street,' MacKenzie said with a look so penetrating that it was almost a glare. 'Please explain to Mr Scougall and myself your reasons for returning to Sir Lachlan's lodgings at such a late hour.'

'I can assure you both,' Hope said, almost whispering, 'that I had nothing to do with the dreadful death of our dear friend.

The reason I returned is of… a most delicate nature, which, if it was to become public, has the power to cause much pain to my dear wife and family.'

'I will do my best to withhold the details from the Crown Officer. Now tell us, how long you have been acquainted with Smith's servant girl?'

Scougall, almost unable to bear the tension of the interrogation, felt himself start to tremble even although he was a mere observer.

Hope closed his eyes and his large Adam's apple made a number of journeys up and down before he placed both his plump hands on the table – the fat, soft hands of a minister. He tried to recover his composure, made a brief prayer to God, and told MacKenzie and Scougall his story.

'After we parted, I made my way down Fish Market Wynd and entered the Targe Tavern, where I waited for perhaps an hour. I then retraced my steps to Sir Lachlan's lodgings. You must understand, Mr MacKenzie, Mr Scougall, the Devil had caught me off-guard after too much wine and had inflamed my passion. Besides, Mrs Hope has, how shall I put it, little interest in easing my cares. There was only one thing on my mind as I re-entered Smith's house. I have a particular weakness, gentlemen. May God forgive me – yes, a particular weakness. Peggy had left the door on the ground floor open for me. I climbed the stairs and on reaching the first floor where Smith and his family have their residence, I heard the door being opened. I hastened onto the next floor as quietly as I could. Peggy's room is at the top of the house and there she was waiting for me. God forgive me, for I did lose the world when I took her in my arms. Afterwards, I lay a while, listening to my heart beat with such vigour I feared it might burst. I am no longer a young man. I heard the Tron Kirk bell strike three times and left the young lady to her slumber.

As I came down the stairs, I heard footsteps coming from Sir Lachlan's chambers. I did not want to be seen so I hid in the shadows. The figure descended in an instant. I cannot say who it was. All I saw was the sweep of a dark cloak. I waited until I heard the person leave the building and then made my way down and escaped into the night.'

'Could you say if the figure you saw was a man or a woman?' asked MacKenzie.

'I supposed it was a man.'

'There was nothing else you noticed about the figure?'

'Nothing – it was very dark.'

MacKenzie continued to stare intently at the minister, his face revealing no hint of his private emotion, for the minister's words had triggered the recollection of another midnight tryst, many years before. Desire, or the memory of desire, returned, as it did less now; the feeling still cut through him like a knife. He shut his eyes for a moment, then turned to Scougall.

'Come, Davie, we have taken up enough of Mr Hope's time. He has sermons to write!'

'My account will not pass beyond these walls, will it, MacKenzie?' asked the minister.

'I will do my best, Mr Hope, but I cannot promise.'

Hope placed his hand on MacKenzie's knee and his eyes seemed to implore him.

The two lawyers were shown out of the manse by a servant and as they walked back towards their horses, MacKenzie said with a smile, 'Davie, I did warn you that I might launch a ferocious attack.'

'I had not imagined you would address a man of God in such a manner,' murmured Scougall. 'Nor that Mr Hope would confess so readily to his sins. How did you know he was seen returning to Sir Lachlan's lodgings?'

'I did not know: I supposed. If you had made a close

examination of the footwear of the guests you would have noticed that Mr Hope was the only person wearing buckled shoes. When you meet a man, always pay as much attention to his feet as to his face – you will learn much. This fact, together with knowledge of the character of our good minister, left me convinced that the person seen by Mr Smith on the stairs was Hope. It is well known in certain circles that he has strong passions after drink and his wife is not obliging. But alas, we have discovered the identity of one figure only to find ourselves with another night prowler to identify.'

'How do you know that Mr Hope is telling the truth sir?' asked Scougall, still more impressed by MacKenzie's observational skills. 'And why would Peggy consent to lie with such a man?'

'We do not know for certain, Davie, but then, there is nothing that we can know for certain. I will talk with Peggy later today. I am sure that, with a little persuasion, she will provide us with information which may or may not corroborate the minister's account. As for her apparent predilection for men of the Kirk – such men have an appeal for some women. No doubt, Hope provided her with something in return. Now I must visit the Parliament House to talk with Mr Stirling and you must visit Mr Primrose and enlist his assistance in drawing up a list of Sir Lachlan's creditors. I ask that you take great care in producing it. Let us meet on Leith Links at three o'clock.'

CHAPTER 9
A Round on the Links

SCOUGALL STOOD MOTIONLESS, head down, eyes fixed on the small ball on the ground between his feet. He slowly raised his club, then swung in a long graceful arc, striking the ball high into the clear blue sky. He watched it fade to the right and kept his eyes on it until it came to rest.

'It is an honour to watch you swing a golf club,' said MacKenzie, who placed his own ball on the ground and struck it in a less dignified fashion. It sliced to the right, bouncing about eighty yards away and landing in some longer grass. As they headed off towards MacKenzie's ball, he enquired how Scougall had fared with Primrose.

'I found him in the Advocate's Library preparing a case. He provided me with an inventory of Sir Lachlan's legal papers and a list of creditors which he had completed for the case against Menzies, and then I went straight to Mr Smith's house, where Hector MacLean gave me access to his father's documents. I spent the next hour closely examining them and am pleased to inform you that they are all present.'

'Interesting. It would seem that our killer did not find what he was looking for. What of the list of creditors?'

'I will show it to you later,' replied Scougall. 'There are twenty-two major creditors.'

'I too have made profitable use of my time. I spoke again

with Mr Stirling and he revealed the contents of Lawtie's report on Sir Lachlan's death. The cause of death was indeed poison, most likely that which is used to destroy vermin. The appearance of the corpse apparently bore all the hallmarks of this deadly agent.'

MacKenzie played his second shot, making better contact with the ball and sending it high into the sky. As they strode off towards Scougall's ball he continued: 'I also visited the house of Sir David Dunbar to determine the veracity of Ann MacLean's account. Dunbar was a loyal supporter of King Charles during the Civil Wars. Sir Lachlan and he have been close friends since they spent time in exile together on the Continent. Sir David was at his country seat near Haddington, but I was entertained by his daughter, who assured me that Ann did spend the entire evening with her. She described the terrible scene when Gregor McIan broke the news of her father's death. On my way out, I struck up conversation with the Dunbar family coachman, a fellow Highlander from Ross-shire. I learned, after slipping him a few pennies, that he had taken Ann to the Pleasance on the evening of her visit, to meet George Scott, an officer in Johnstone's regiment. The coachman was told to wait for her. She spent about an hour at Scott's lodgings, from around nine o'clock until ten, and then returned to Dunbar's house.'

'If that is so, she could not have played any part in her father's murder,' said Scougall as he addressed his ball and hit a second glorious shot. 'But what of the character of George Scott?'

'As far as I know, Scott is a diligent soldier. We must find out more about him. I believe that Sir Lachlan stood firmly against Ann's marriage to him. Scott has little money and few political connections. I will speak to my kinsman Kenneth Chisholm, who serves in Johnstone's Regiment.'

MacKenzie was preparing to play his third shot when he

was distracted by shouts in the distance. Archibald Stirling's servant was calling for him. When the old man reached them, he stood for a few seconds to catch his breath before being able to speak.

'An urgent message from Mr Stirling, sir. He wishes that you meet him as soon as possible at the Nor' Loch. A body has been found!'

CHAPTER 10
The Nor' Loch in the Gloaming

BY THE TIME MacKenzie and Scougall arrived it was already growing dark and the black mass of the Castle Rock cast the water of the Nor' Loch into shadow. After spending some time wandering along the muddy shore, they spotted Stirling and a small entourage, including the physician, Lawtie, and several lugubrious looking members of the Town Guard, at the bottom of the steep slope which led from the houses on the High Street down to the dank water of the loch. As they approached they saw that the figures stood around a body at the water's edge.

'John, Mr Scougall,' Stirling greeted them, 'I am sorry to have summoned you to this dismal place at such an hour. The body was found by two young boys this afternoon. It was lying face down in the shallows. Mr Lawtie is making an examination. It appears that the deceased is James Jossie, an apothecary in Steel's Close. I believe his death may be linked to Sir Lachlan's, for only this morning I ordered my two men to talk with all the apothecaries concerning their supplies of poison. Perhaps Sir Lachlan's killer obtained his deadly agent from Mr Jossie and then dispatched him lest he was identified.' Stirling looked pleased with himself.

Lawtie rose from his examination of the corpse, his small eyes giving him the appearance of an animal emerging from a burrow. 'This has been a most savage attack, gentlemen. The deceased was stabbed with a blade which pierced the heart. He must have bled to death in seconds. Blood loss has been immense. We must transport the body to a more suitable location for a full post-mortem. Mr Stirling, you will have a report as usual by tomorrow. I expect payment will be as prompt? I am still waiting to be paid for the last one I penned for your office.'

'Don't worry, Lawtie. You will be paid,' said Stirling as the physician made his departure into the gloom.

'Did anyone see anything relating to the attack?' asked MacKenzie.

'No one has come forward as yet, John.'

'May I examine the corpse?'

MacKenzie walked over and looked down at a face caught in the grimace of death. Scougall could not find it in himself to come closer, and stared instead towards the open fields to the north of Edinburgh. There was just a thin line of light on the horizon. The image of Sir Lachlan under the linen sheet filled his mind. He asked God to give him strength to turn and look upon the old apothecary so that he might be able to aid MacKenzie in some way. But he could not bring himself to do so and his eyes remained fixed on the fading view.

Stirling looked glumly at MacKenzie.

'Have you any further thoughts about Sir Lachlan's death, John? My enquiries have as yet led nowhere. As you know, I have a number of detailed narratives. Even taken together, they tell me next to nothing. It remains possible that the chief may have committed suicide and that the death of Mr Jossie is entirely unrelated.'

'I am giving the matter my complete attention, Archibald. Mr Scougall and I will make some more enquiries in the city and then I intend to travel to the Highlands for Sir Lachlan's funeral. I am confident that by the time he is laid to rest in the family tomb we will know the identity of his killer. Do you have any intelligence of Glenbeg's whereabouts?'

'Indeed. I have been informed of his presence in Perth, but that he has since left the town, no doubt heading for the mountains, where he is at home. He will be difficult to locate. Orders have been sent to the sheriff for his arrest. I am sure he has played some part in these terrible events. May I suggest we return to the safety of the city, gentlemen, for it growing dark.'

'We will follow in a few minutes,' replied MacKenzie.

The town guards, an unshaven crew dressed in ill-fitting uniforms, lifted the corpse onto a wooden stretcher and departed with Stirling eastwards, for taking a direct route up the steep hill that led to the High Street was not possible with a dead body.

'This affair grows blacker by the hour, Davie.'

'Then you think the apothecary's death is connected with the killing of Sir Lachlan?'

'Nothing can be proved, as yet, but I suggest we pay a visit to the shop in Steel's Close as soon as we can. Stirling may soon remember to send one of his men and I fear that any evidence left by the murderer may be misunderstood.'

The two men followed a pathway beside the water, stumbling on loose stones in the darkness. At the foot of the Castle Rock, the path wound its way up the side of the hill. Towering tenements loomed like a cliff of sheer rock, dotted with a few bright eyes, the windows of those who had tallow to burn.

'Tomorrow we must make the most of our time. I have some work to complete at the Session in the morning and I daresay there are a few unfinished instruments that need your attention in your office. I will speak with Kenneth Chisholm about George Scott and I also wish to probe the knowledge of some of our lordships on the bench. They may appear decrepit but they have long memories and I want to glean further information about some of the characters we are concerned with. In the afternoon I have a social engagement. The Earl of Boortree's eldest daughter is to be married and a celebration is being held at Boortree House near Dalkeith. The Earl is an old friend – I have acted as his legal adviser for many years. The following day we leave for the Highlands to attend Sir Lachlan's funeral at Glenshieldaig.'

Scougall tried to conceal the fact that he was unnerved at the prospect of such a journey.

'Why must we attend, sir?'

'Did you not intend to pay your respects to Sir Lachlan's family at his funeral?'

'I had not thought, sir,' stammered Scougall.

'It will be an education for you. Put aside your law books and your golf clubs. We travel to Glenshieldaig.'

Scougall was silent for the rest of the climb, his mind filled with thoughts of the Highlands. He was steeped in tales, told him by his grandmother, which conjured up visions of the Highlands as a savage territory roamed by bands of murderers and in the grip of Popery. But he had no choice, he must do as he was ordered. Despite his apprehension an excitement stirred within him at the prospect of the first real journey of his life. He had never travelled further than twenty miles from Edinburgh.

CHAPTER 11

Back at the Apothecary's Shop

IT WAS PITCH dark by the time they reached John Jossie's small shop at the bottom of Steel's Close. The lane was only about eight feet wide and the walls on either side soared to a height of sixty feet. MacKenzie pushed the door and found, to his surprise, that it was open.

'Davie, go down to John Anderson's tavern and get some candles so we can see something.'

MacKenzie entered the shop and stood in absolute darkness. Although he could see nothing, his other senses were stimulated. There was a strange smell, a mixture of chemicals and spices, which he had always associated with such places. He inhaled deeply – the odour of cloves was strongest – he detected a hint of almonds. He listened intently, but there was nothing. He was about to move further into the apothecary's when he thought he heard a slight noise – the hairs on his neck rose. He sensed that he was not alone, that the sound he had heard was of someone breathing. He stood stock still, his senses taut. But it was gone. Perhaps it had only been his imagination. He began to inch forward into the blackness with his arms stretched out. The sound of his own heart thudding seemed to fill the room.

He stopped again and did not move for a couple of minutes, standing so still that his legs began to shake. They were still tired after the steep ascent from the Nor' Loch. Suddenly, there was the same sound again – unmistakeably someone else was there, within a few feet of him! His hand slowly moved round to his belt and took hold of the small dagger he always carried with him. He listened but there was only silence. Then there it was again – he was sure that he heard stifled breathing, perhaps a foot moving on the floor. Should he address the figure? But that would indicate exactly where he was and the intruder might be on him in seconds. Better to wait for Davie to return. Where in heaven's name was that confounded clerk! No doubt waiting his turn in a busy tavern, unwilling to push in front of anyone. He must teach that boy how to act more forcefully.

Time seemed to have stopped. At last a candle appeared through the window. As Scougall entered, MacKenzie shouted, 'Get down!' At that moment, a figure thrust into Scougall, knocking him to the floor, and was off out of the door and into the close. Fortunately the candle remained lit. MacKenzie ran to Scougall's inert form.

'Are you all right, Davie?' Scougall was shaken but had not received a blow from a weapon. 'Quick, can you get up, we must follow!' shouted MacKenzie.

Both men ran out of the shop only to see a figure turning onto the High Street, fifty yards away. By the time they had reached the street their assailant was lost in the crowds. It was still early in the evening and there was much activity as shopkeepers closed up for the day and the thirsty townsfolk sought lubrication for their throats.

'I have not the speed of my younger years, Davie,' said MacKenzie, bending over and trying to recover his breath.

'I was always the slowest runner of my age at the burgh school,' Scougall confessed.

'A sorry pair, indeed!' gasped MacKenzie. 'But all is not lost. Let us return and see what we can find.'

MacKenzie lit another candle from the one Scougall had retrieved from the floor and held it up so he could see something of the shop they stood in. It was but one small room – a door and window on one wall, boxes and pieces of equipment down the left, a bench and shelves on which bottles, glasses and pots rested on the wall facing the door, and bookshelves on the right. The floor was wooden and very dirty with all kinds of debris strewn across it.

MacKenzie crouched on his hands and knees, holding the candle a few inches from his nose. As he made a meticulous examination, he did not utter a word. Scougall stood holding his candle up so that he could read the labels of the exotic ingredients that made up the everyday materials of the apothecary: rose-water, antimony, mercury, cinnamon. Scougall wondered what it felt like to be poisoned and face the last moments of life in terror, panic, pain… before being swept up into the arms of God.

After about ten minutes on the floor, MacKenzie broke the silence:

'Now I think it is time for us to retire for the night. I am finished here. Stirling's men will no doubt inspect the place tomorrow. I daresay they will be very confused with what they find. But I have enough for now. Let us return to our chambers. I wish to reflect on the events of today and what has happened here tonight. I'm sure the hour is already late for you, Davie.'

Scougall nodded tired agreement. The thought of bed was most welcome.

CHAPTER 12
Breakfast at MacKenzie's Chambers

'AT LAST, DAVIE! I've been waiting for you these thirty minutes. It is already 9 o'clock and we have much to do.'

Scougall had only recently dragged himself from bed and his uncombed hair stood at an odd angle on one side. His eyes were puffy with sleep and his clothes had evidently been carelessly thrown on.

'I'm sorry, sir, but the exertions of yestreen have taken the spirit out of me and I awoke feeling stiff and sore.'

'Come now, a climb up from the Nor' Loch and a little scuffle in an apothecary's shop! Sit yourself down and have some breakfast while we talk about last night.'

Scougall sat at the table where the advocate had just taken his breakfast. He poured a beaker of milk from a jug and tore off a piece of fresh bread that MacKenzie's servant Meg had set in front of him. She said something to him in Gaelic. In response he could do no more than smile and nod his head. This was the first time he had been entertained in MacKenzie's Edinburgh chambers in Libberton's Wynd. A very modest set of rooms, but homely. The room in which they were eating was where MacKenzie both dined and worked. A large table rested against the wall at one end, where Scougall now sat. At the other was a desk covered with documents. A fire burned in the hearth. Among the bookcases that lined the room, there was space only for a single portrait. Scougall noticed that the subject bore a striking resemblance to Elizabeth. He was sure she had entered his dreams during the night.

'Is that a painting of Elizabeth, sir?'

'No, Davie – that is my wife, also Elizabeth. She died following my daughter's birth. It was a hard time for me, the hardest of my life...'

The image of her beautiful dead body came back to MacKenzie and, with it, a wave of nausea. Once more he stood at the edge of the pit. He shook himself. He had no time for such self-indulgence just now. Unaccountably to Scougall, he brought his fist down hard on the desk he was standing beside. The black feelings returned to their lair.

'I must confess I am baffled by the events in Mr Jossie's shop last night. What did you make of it all?' Scougall asked.

'I expect Jossie's killer returned to recover something.'

Scougall munched on a piece of bread.

'But what?'

'Something he had left there by mistake?'

'Or she. What do you make of this?'

MacKenzie pulled an object from his pocket and held it up between his thumb and forefinger. Scougall identified it as a small piece of jewellery, apparently made from silver. A somewhat crude example of the silversmith's art, it appeared to be a representation of a herring.

'It looks like a brooch, sir.'

'Very observant, Davie. Have you come across anything like it before? After all, you are a native of a burgh which depends on the catching of fish for its livelihood.'

'Indeed, sir, but I recall never having seen a piece of jewellery like this before. Mr Grave, our minister, has often warned the women of our parish to turn their eyes against such frivolous things!'

'The problem is that we have no way of knowing if this

brooch, which I found on the floor under Jossie's work bench, belonged to him, to a customer, or to the murderer. The killer may have returned to recover it or for some other reason. I examined Jossie's ledger and found the pages covering the last four days of business had been torn out. Jossie was known as a diligent apothecary who kept a careful inventory noting all the products he bought and sold. Our assailant, it seems, returned to destroy this evidence and has successfully done so, but may have left us with another clue to his or her identity.'

'But why would this person have bought the poison and not sought it elsewhere anonymously, or stolen it? It seems a terrible risk to have walked into an apothecary's shop and purchased it,' said Scougall.

As the young notary took a large draught of cool milk, MacKenzie nodded thoughtfully.

'There were also clear indications that the murder occurred at the door of the shop – bloodstains on the wooden floor and on the door. The killer must have stabbed Jossie through the heart as soon as the door was opened. There was no sign of a struggle or fight. Death or unconsciousness must have been instantaneous.'

Scougall stopped eating. All this talk of death had killed his appetite. The image of the old apothecary slumped on the shore of the Nor' Loch came back to him. He wrenched himself away from the thought.

'Do you believe that a woman would be capable of committing such a crime, sir?' he asked.

'It is possible. Women can show great strength when the moment requires. During my years in court I have witnessed many women who have committed murder. I remember a particular case in 1666, the year of the great fire in London. Janet Webster was found guilty of a series of murders, all committed using utensils from her kitchen. She disposed of the bodies at night, dragging them across her rig to the woods beyond and burying them under the cover of the trees. Women kill less often than men, but we cannot dismiss Ann MacLean on the basis of her sex alone. The apothecary was old and infirm, and most likely caught by surprise. A small dagger can do much damage when wielded swiftly.'

Scougall's eyes wandered back to the portrait – he did not believe that a woman could be involved in such atrocities.

'Now, there was another matter which I wanted to discuss with you this morning,' MacKenzie continued. 'Sir Lachlan's creditors.'

'Yes, sir.' Scougall rummaged in a leather pouch and handed him a document.

MacKenzie unfolded the sheet of paper and his brow furrowed as he read out loud:

'A list of the creditors of Sir Lachlan MacLean of Glenshieldaig drawn up by Mr Francis Primrose, advocate 12th April 1686. The Earl of Argyll £10,000, (4 bonds), James Sovrack £10,000 (3 bonds), the Earl of Perth 10,000 merks (2 bonds), Sir George Lockhart 10,000 merks (4 bonds), Lord Prestonhall 8,000 merks (4 bonds), Sir Thomas Stewart of Grandtully £7,000 (3 bonds), Alexander Hamilton £6,000 (4 bonds), Sir Henry Ashurst in England £6,000 (3 bonds), Sir William Menzies 5,000 merks (2 bonds), Colin Campbell of Carwhin, Writer to the Signet, £5,000 (3 bonds), Mr Foster in Dundee 4,000 merks (2 bonds), John Smith, merchant in Edinburgh £6,000 (3 bonds), Angus MacLean of Ardloch £5,000 (2 bonds), Major Duncan MacLean 3,000 merks (2 bonds), John MacKenzie, advocate in Edinburgh, £2,000 (2 bonds), Francis Primrose, advocate, 1,000 merks (1 bond), John Gledstanes, merchant in Edinburgh, 1,000 merks (1 bond), Robert Andrew, merchant in Edinburgh, 1,000 merks (1 bond), Captain James MacLean £1,000 (1 bond), Mr

Alexander MacLean, writer in Edinburgh, 1,000 merks (2 bonds), Mr John Hope, minister, 500 merks (1 bond).

'An exhaustive list, Davie. *Bha iasad a ghabhail's a thoirt riamh air feadh an t-saoghail*, as we say in Gaelic.'

Scougall waited for MacKenzie to translate his words.

'Borrowing and lending were always in fashion! These debts have brought much trouble to Sir Lachlan and the MacLeans of Glenshieldaig. Did you know that lending with interest was not legal in Scotland until Acts of Parliament were passed after the break with Rome in 1560? Your reformers have much to answer for.'

'It is surely the character of the debtor that is to blame,' said Scougall indignantly. 'All the men on the list have lent in good faith and deserve a reasonable return on their money. Surely the responsibility lies with the man who borrows and who cannot repay, and then borrows again to repay his first debt, and then again – especially if it is for superfluous luxuries. I always make sure my outstanding bills are paid in full at the end of every quarter.'

'Let us not commence a debate on the ethics of moneylending, Davie. It is perhaps a subject we could return to when we have discovered the identity of the killer.'

Both men fell silent. MacKenzie rose from his desk and began to wander round the chamber deep in thought.

'You were a creditor, sir. I am afraid my eyes passed over your name when I first glanced at the paper,' said Scougall hesitantly.

'Yes, that is so, Sir Lachlan owed me a few pounds. But you might say I have already written the sum off. He did not often ask to borrow from me, perhaps realising I could not provide him with sound legal advice if I was too concerned with the recovery of my money – I regarded this as a mark of respect. I could live with a sum of two thousand pounds

Scots – but two thousand pounds Sterling would have been a different matter.'

'And Mr Primrose and Mr Hope were also creditors of the chief,' commented Scougall.

'Yes. It is no surprise that Primrose was a creditor. Sir Lachlan has borrowed from every lawyer whose hand he has shaken. Many advocates and even some notaries have been forced to take him to court over the years. This list unfortunately only comprises those who are owed money now. It gives no hint of the long and tortuous route by which these debts have been bought and sold, before coming into the hands of the present owners, or of the many court cases that have been fought against Sir Lachlan for the recovery of debt. But it is all we have. The sum that Hope is owed is not great and may have been in return for services rendered.'

'What services do you mean, sir?'

'I am only thinking aloud, Davie: a man prone to powerful desires of the flesh may have found it useful to have had some firepower as a back-up – firepower to threaten anyone who might be inclined to inform his wife. A Highland chief is still viewed by many as a useful ally and worth paying for.'

MacKenzie sat down opposite the young notary, once more calm and focused.

'Davie, what do you make of James Sovrack?'

'I have never heard the name before.'

'Nor I. It is the only name on the list I do not recognise. The sum owed to this individual was very substantial.'

'Perhaps a merchant from London?' suggested Scougall.

'Possibly. Sir Lachlan made many journeys there over the years. Or he may be from France, the United Provinces or even Dublin. As I have already told you, I travel to Dalkeith this afternoon to attend the betrothal celebrations of Boortree's daughter. While I am busy there you must make yourself useful. I have a task for you to complete before we leave for the Highlands tomorrow morning. I want you to ask the Edinburgh writers of your acquaintance, including the venerable Mr Dallas, if they have heard of this James Sovrack. You might also question some of the merchants, for if he is a businessman of any standing they would presumably have heard of him. Then you may return to your office, but make sure you are prepared for an early start tomorrow.'

The door opened and Elizabeth MacKenzie entered dressed in a white gown. She sat at the table beside Scougall. Her proximity caused his thoughts about the murders to melt away. He was delighted to see her again.

'Good morning father, Mr Scougall. I hope you do not mind if I join you for breakfast?'

'Of course not, my dear. Davie and I have just completed our business. I must be off to the Session. Davie, please finish your breakfast in the company of my daughter.'

MacKenzie kissed her and left the chamber before Scougall had finished the mouthful he was chewing. Elizabeth poured some milk and cut a slice of bread. He was desperately trying to think of something to say, but as usual in such circumstances nothing sprang to mind that did not seem ridiculous.

'Are you always so quiet, Mr Scougall?' she asked.

'I fear that the range of my conversation is not broad, Miss MacKenzie. I can only discourse freely on a few subjects – the art of the notary public and golf. Such things might easily become tiresome,' he responded, infuriated at his own lack of social finesse.

'Do not worry, Mr Scougall,' Elizabeth replied, 'I am sure that I can talk for us both. But let us forget such pleasantries.' She pulled her chair closer to the table and her voice fell to a whisper. 'I want to know more about the murders. Everyone in town is talking about them. All my friends think I can supply them with the details they crave because I'm the daughter of John MacKenzie. But my father tells me nothing, absolutely nothing! He keeps too much to himself. It is always the same – never sharing his cares with me, and I know he has many. Please tell me what you have learned about the murders of Sir Lachlan and Mr Jossie.'

Scougall was surprised by the realisation that he did, after all, have something to say that would interest Elizabeth.

'Your father is doing all he can to determine the identity of the killer, but does not have sufficient evidence to come to any definite conclusions. Last night, after we were summoned to the Nor' Loch by Mr Stirling, we returned to Jossie's shop and disturbed an intruder who knocked me to the ground and fled down the close. Unfortunately your father and I were not fast enough to catch him and he escaped.'

Scougall basked in the knowledge of having captured Elizabeth's full attention.

'We returned to the shop and,' he couldn't help embellishing his own role in the events of the previous evening, 'your father and I made an examination of the scene. Your father thinks Jossie was killed at the door. He found what might be an important clue, a brooch in the shape of a fish which was possibly dropped by the killer during the murder of the apothecary.'

'You must find the person who has lost this brooch, Mr Scougall!'

'It would seem so, although I have seen nothing of its like before – it was about this size.' Scougall indicated with his fingers the dimensions of the brooch. 'It appears to be a herring – a silver herring – a silver darling.' The word 'darling' seemed to linger on his lips and his face began to colour.

'And are you knowledgeable about the jewellers' art?' asked Elizabeth.

'No! My mother does not wear jewellery and she has forbidden my sisters from doing so.'

'That is a great shame for your sisters and your mother, Mr Scougall. Perhaps I can help. I am acquainted with most of the city's jewellers… I can see you disapprove.'

Scougall's eyes were taken with the silver chain that hung round her neck. How wonderful it looked! Perhaps Mr Grave was wrong in his pronouncements against such items. He shook his head in confusion.

'I will ask my friends if they have seen any such brooches. We meet this afternoon. I shall be in Edinburgh for a few days to look after my father's chambers while he is in the Highlands and to keep Meg company. If I find out anything I will send you a note. That is, if you do not mind.'

'Yes, of course.'

Scougall was greatly pleased at the thought of receiving a written communication from Elizabeth.

'Now, you must excuse me. I hope it will not be long till we meet again.'

CHAPTER 13

An Engagement Feast

MACKENZIE MADE HIS way on horseback down the long avenue of newly planted trees. He could not help feeling somewhat bemused by the splendour of the Boortree family's new abode, which had been designed for them by Sir William Bruce. The old castle had been an impressive building for its time and had provided more than enough room for the large entourage of servants and kinsmen who were in permanent residence. The new mansion was on an entirely different scale: there were perhaps three times the number of rooms and an equivalent escalation in the number of household servants. MacKenzie was worried about the impact of this on his friend's finances. The Earl had been unable to secure sufficient funds in Edinburgh and had been forced to borrow from London merchants and lawyers at high interest rates. A splendid edifice had been constructed – of that there could be no doubt – but it rested on very flimsy financial foundations, and any crisis in the family, or decline in the Earl's income, could bring significant problems.

MacKenzie had advised his lordship on many occasions to restrain his spending, but his advice had gone unheeded. Had MacKenzie not seen the kind of houses being built by the English aristocracy around London, his lordship had argued? How could he be expected to entertain the noblemen of England in a cold and leaking edifice like Boortree Castle? It was unthinkable. How was he to marry his daughter to the son of an English aristocrat if he could not demonstrate the wealth and prestige of the Scottish nobility? It was a matter of national pride and would further the union between the kingdoms of Scotland and England.

MacKenzie chuckled to himself. He could not understand the unedifying attempts of Scottish nobles to imitate their southern neighbours. They should remember that Scotland was a small and poor country. Borrowing on this scale to secure an English marriage could only endanger the future of her noble houses and the independence of the kingdom – but the attractions of the Court in London were great. He remembered his first visit to the city, in 1651, on his way to the Continent to study law at Leiden. He had enjoyed a blissful summer in the English capital – a time of wine, women and song; he had seen with his own eyes the beauties of the day and had lost his virginity to an unemployed actress. It seemed like another world, another life – long before he had met his wife – an early chapter of joy.

Putting such thoughts from his mind, MacKenzie climbed the steps to the entrance. He was, after all, attending a celebration and not a meeting to discuss the Earl's finances. As he approached, he had counted twelve rectangular windows on each floor. The corners were adorned with high pillars of a classical style and a small portico surrounded the front door. The overall effect was one of symmetry and proportion. To his taste it was a little dull. He preferred the spirited vernacular design of his own much smaller dwelling.

MacKenzie was welcomed by a servant dressed in English livery who spoke with a southern accent. English servants – another needless expense, MacKenzie thought. The entrance hall was impressive: two marble staircases rose on left and right, curving round to meet at a doorway above. A cupola allowed an infusion of light so that the ornate classical carvings and huge portraits of flamboyantly dressed men and women came to life.

He was led into a richly decorated reception room where the celebration was being held. It was almost full; conversation rose and fell above the music of a virginal. A small man in a large wig, dressed in a long blue velvet coat came forward to welcome him.

'John MacKenzie, my favourite lawyer! I have missed our little discussions these last two months.'

He shook MacKenzie's hand vigorously and looked up at him, for the Earl was not much more than five feet tall.

'My Lordship, I too have missed your company, but I must first congratulate you on your daughter's engagement. May I say that the exquisite web you have spun has caught the English fly.'

'My future son-in-law would not take too kindly to being called a fly.' The two men laughed. 'Now John, you must congratulate Helen yourself. Here she is.'

A young woman dressed in a magnificent scarlet gown appeared from behind her father. MacKenzie kissed her and passed on his good wishes. After a few pleasantries she ran off to talk with other late arrivals who appeared more interesting than an old Edinburgh advocate.

'What is the news from town, John? The murder of Sir Lachlan is the only subject of conversation in these isolated parts of the Lothians. Are they close to catching anyone? I must keep my voice down, for Ann MacLean is here with Dunbar's daughter. Her brother, who I must say is a very serious young man, is also in attendance.'

'I fear the Crown Officer's men make little progress, your lordship, but I am devoting much of my own time to discover the perpetrator of this dreadful crime. I have been asked by the kin to investigate on their behalf. After all, I was with Sir Lachlan the night before he was killed.'

'Here John, take a glass of wine.' A silver tray was presented to MacKenzie by a smartly dressed servant. 'Let us drink to the swift apprehension of the person responsible.'

MacKenzie and the Earl raised their glasses. 'Alas, I must make myself a useful host. If I do not speak to you later – there are after all three hundred guests here today – we will meet next month to discuss business as usual. Until then, John.'

MacKenzie looked around, nodding now and again at guests he recognised. He was not in the mood for general conversation. There were only two people in the room with whom he wanted to speak. At last he caught sight of Ann MacLean in the throng and made his way towards her.

She was dressed in black and gave a nervous smile as MacKenzie greeted her. He had already met Isabella Dunbar and he took her hand. 'I am George Scott,' said the tall man standing beside her.

'Of the family of Drumsheugh?' asked MacKenzie.

'That is right, sir.'

'This is John MacKenzie – who was my father's legal man in Edinburgh,' Ann said.

'And how are you, Ann?' asked MacKenzie. He was a little surprised that she and her brother would attend such a gathering so soon after their father's death.

'I am well, Mr MacKenzie, though I do not relish the long journey to Glenshieldaig. I will be pleased to return south when my father has been buried.'

'Of course,' said MacKenzie, turning his intense gaze from Ann to George Scott and back again.

'Is there any word from Mr Stirling? There are rumours that the demise of an apothecary is somehow connected with my father's death.' Ann's tone was cold, as if she was forcing herself to make polite conversation.

'I fear that Mr Stirling's investigations are still at an early stage, but Mr Scougall and I are putting our wits to the test and I think we are making some headway.'

'Why should you and Mr Scougall be so presumptuous to take on such a role? With whose authority do you act?'

'I act with the authority of your own kin, as appointed by your brother. I was also your father's friend, Ann, and it is my duty as his friend to do all I can to bring his killer to justice.'

'That is very noble of you, Mr MacKenzie,' interjected George Scott, trying to defuse the tension. 'I am sure that Ann did not mean to offend – she is still very upset.'

'I understand. Perhaps I should not have spoken about your father's death at what is, after all, a celebration. But, how shall I put this, Sir Lachlan's demise must be an advantage to you both!'

Ann MacLean's face reddened and a flash of fury lit up her eyes. She took her friend by the hand and dragged her away. 'Come, Isabella, I care not to be cross-examined. Mr MacKenzie should be mindful of his status.'

'I am sorry, Mr Scott – my questioning was perhaps a little rough.' Scott was above six feet in height and dressed smartly. MacKenzie noticed the glint of a small silver dagger hanging beneath his waistcoat. He was not going to let this opportunity slip.

'Mr Scott. I believe you and Ann are soon to be married?'

The young soldier was rattled and did not answer for a few moments.

'I believe you intend to throw me with your lawyer's manner, Mr MacKenzie. But I am not in court and I do not have to say anything on that matter.'

'I must apologise. An old lawyer's habit which I should

retain for the Session.' Scott had more wit than MacKenzie had anticipated. 'Then if I may ask you a less intrusive question. I have heard that you follow the profession of soldier?'

'You are correct, sir.'

'Do you intend to continue with your career in the military?'

'It is the only one I know, but my days of fighting for foreign kings are over. I wish to take a commission in an English regiment.'

'Very patriotic,' replied MacKenzie sardonically.

'Our family estates are still saddled with debt and I must earn money somewhere.'

'Of course, Mr Scott – a problem faced by many families. If I may ask but one further question. Is it true that Sir Lachlan once threatened to kill you?'

Scott hesitated for an instant.

'You have been well informed, sir. We had many disagreements and on one occasion he did say that force might be used if I did not stop seeing Ann. Sir Lachlan often spoke before he thought. He viewed my family as socially inferior and our match as dishonourable. For him love had nothing to do with it.'

'And life is now much more agreeable for you since his death?'

Scott flinched visibly.

'I must now negotiate with a new chief. I do not know if he will be any more willing to accept me as brother-in-law as his father was to welcome me as son-in-law.'

'I wish you well, Mr Scott.' MacKenzie bowed his head and took his leave, for he had spotted Primrose out of the corner of his eye, and he wanted to talk with him.

CHAPTER 14
Scougall Takes an Evening Stroll

DAVIE SCOUGALL CAREFULLY wrote the final clause of the instrument of sasine that he had been working on for most of the afternoon in his small office. It was unusual for him to take so long over a document. He normally focused all his attention on the work at hand and was able to complete a fine instrument in an hour. But his mind was distracted. So much had happened to him in the last few days and he was trying to make some sense of it all. He felt that he had crammed more into the last week than the previous twenty-four years. During his long apprenticeship with Mr Dallas, he had divided his time between ten-hour sessions with the pen and a few hours at the golf in the early evening. Dallas had been a hard taskmaster and had demanded unstinting accuracy, but he had become fond of him and it had been a pleasant visit that morning. Those days now seemed years away; a life belonging to a stranger, although it was only three weeks since MacKenzie had walked into his office, introduced himself, and informed him that he required the services of a reliable writer and that he, Davie Scougall, came highly recommended by the venerable notary Mr Hugh Dallas. He had been overjoyed at the prospect of regular work for such an important advocate. But since then his life had been turned upside down and there had been no time to sit back and reflect. His agitated mind was telling him to relax and spend a few more hours on the Links. But how could he when he was on the trail of a murderer? And now he was to travel with MacKenzie into the Highlands to attend the funeral of a chief. He thought it might be prudent to send his mother and father a letter telling them where he was going, lest something should happen to him on the journey. He dared not think what his mother would say when she heard about his destination. His grandmother would be appalled. It was she, after all, who had filled his young head with tales of lawless clans. He must find some time after his return to visit them all in Musselburgh.

After penning a quick note to his parents, he put down his quill and placed the documents he had been working on in a small cabinet, which he locked, then pulled on a rather threadbare cloak and stepped outside. It was a fine evening. Some fresh air would clear his mind. He often walked down the High Street towards the Palace after work if he was not golfing.

Scougall's tiny office was in the basement of one of the high tenements across from St Giles Kirk. He locked the door, climbed the few steps up to the High Street and looked up at the crown-shaped steeple towering above the Luckenbooths and the Tolbooth. The sky was a perfect blue and he breathed in deeply. He always felt content after a long day's work.

Today, instead of turning left as usual, he made his way uphill in the direction of the Castle and soon found himself at the opening of Steel's Close, where he and MacKenzie had lost sight of the figure from the apothecary's shop the previous night. The sun was slipping low in the sky and the close was now in shadow. He screwed up his eyes and looked down the long passageway between the tenements. Dare he go down and have another look? His first inclination was to forget about it – but was he not the assistant of Mr John MacKenzie, advocate, and an associate of Mr Archibald Stirling, the Crown Officer who acted for the famous Advocate Rosehaugh? Bolstered by such thoughts, he began to make his way slowly past a series of small shops that were closing up for the day, until he found himself outside James Jossie's door. A handwritten note had been attached to it, indicating that the business was closed.

Everything seemed peaceful. Scougall continued down to the hole in the old wall which led to the pathway he had climbed with MacKenzie the night before. He was now back in sunlight and faced with a wonderful view across the Nor' Loch to the Firth of Forth, gleaming silver, rather than its usual grey, with the fields of Fife in the distance. Scougall peered to see if he could catch sight of a mountain in the north, but it was too hazy.

As he was about to climb through the gap in the wall and descend to the path, he stopped in his tracks. A patch of dark red on the stones beneath his foot caught his eye. Scougall shuddered. The image of the apothecary bleeding to death rose in his mind. Had Jossie been dragged here by the murderer? His eyes followed the pathway, looking for more signs of the savagery of the previous day. After a few minutes of scrutiny he found another dried splash of blood three feet further down the track.

He followed the path for about fifty yards until it bifurcated, one branch leading down to the Nor' Loch, the route they had taken the previous night, and the other along the hillside to a precipitous rock face. He found another bloodstain on the latter path, which led along the higher route to end in an area of bushes and shrubs. A few yards off the path, there was a sharp drop. Scougall peered over the edge. The bare rock went straight down for about thirty feet, then a grass slope led to the mirky water of the loch. In all probability this was where Jossie had been thrown to his watery grave. He looked around but could see little indication of disturbance. Jossie must have been dead already and his body dragged along. The killer must have been strong – it was a fair distance from the shop. Surely Ann MacLean would not have been able to carry a body so far, unless aided by George Scott? Or was it Hector MacLean and one of Sir Lachlan's old servants? Scougall imagined each character in turn dragging the old apothecary along the track and throwing him down the slope. Finally he pictured Glenbeg carrying the corpse under his arm and hurling it over the edge.

He retraced his steps and was relieved to find himself back on the High Street amongst other human beings, then walked down the gentle slope towards St Giles, hoping to seek guidance from a higher authority and give thanks for his deliverance the previous night.

He was always impressed with the splendour of the ancient kirk. It was perhaps small in comparison to the great cathedrals of England and France, but for someone who was accustomed to worshipping in a parish church it was a remarkable building. The north façade was a series of projecting gabled chapels and aisles. The crown-shaped steeple reminded him of the Scottish monarchy. He recalled that kings had not lived in Scotland since 1603, when James VI inherited the great English crown from Elizabeth, and had departed south in haste, only to return to his northern kingdom once thereafter. It was a great shame that Scotland had lost its king, but then he reflected on the disastrous policies of James's son, King Charles I, who had tried to shift the Scottish kirk towards popery. Perhaps Scotland was safer without a king! It was at this very spot that Jenny Geddes had thrown her stool.

The image of his grandmother telling the tale of this heroine of the Covenant came to him – one of the clearest memories of his childhood, for the old woman, in the telling, had suddenly seized the very stool she sat on and threatened to throw it across the room. The effect on him and his sisters had been overwhelming. The honest women-folk of Scotland standing up to a king! And now the kirk was officially a cathedral and the seat of a bishop. He hoped dearly that it might become a place of Presbyterian worship again.

The door was open and he went inside. His eyes took a few seconds to adjust to the gloom for it was now almost dark outside and the kirk lit by a few flickering candles. Scougall admired the huge stone pillars supporting the roof. Placing his hand on one, he was reminded of the great age of the church – thousands of folk had worshipped here. He wondered how many had placed their hands on the cold stone like himself.

He was comforted by the atmosphere; the stream of thoughts about the murder of Sir Lachlan, which had upset his daily rhythm, began to recede. There were only a few people inside, each meditating in silence. He sat down on one of the wooden benches, put his hands together, bowed his head, closed his eyes and began to pray: 'Lord give me strength at this difficult time – let me think clearly so I might be of use to Mr MacKenzie. Guide my friend in his pursuit of the truth. Provide him with evidence to bring the person who has sinned against you to justice. Lord, if only you would give me a sign which might help me understand these terrible events, for I am completely at a loss to comprehend the reasons for such heinous crimes.'

Scougall heard someone passing and stopped his prayer. A woman sat down a few rows in front of him. He continued in a soft whisper: 'Lord, I also beseech you – look after me in my journey tomorrow. I know that many Highlanders are godless barbarians and servants of the Antichrist. I ask you, for the sake of my mother and father, to lead me safely through this valley of evil. Always direct me away from sin. Amen.'

As he raised his head, he became aware that there was something familiar about the woman in front of him, yet he could not remember where he had seen her before. He racked his brains, becoming increasingly annoyed with himself. She looked unremarkable enough: middle-aged, soberly dressed, greying hair – a merchant's wife. That was it – she was John Smith's bedfellow!

He was about to move forward and offer his respects when he realised that she too was praying; he thought he could hear her crying quietly into her clasped hands. Yes, he was certain, she was sobbing. It occurred to him that he should go and comfort her but decided against it. She would be displeased to know he had been watching her. Suddenly she rose to leave. Scougall closed his eyes again and bowed his head, pretending to pray. As she passed him in the aisle, he caught a glimpse through his fingers of a distraught face. He listened to the sound of her footsteps as she made her way to the north door.

Scougall was puzzled. It crossed his mind that this was perhaps the sign he had requested from God. Was Mrs Smith involved in this terrible crime? Or was she still coming to terms with the brutal fact that a murder or suicide had taken place under her own roof while she slept? Whatever the reason, MacKenzie would certainly be interested to learn of her agitation and of his discovery on the path. His master was not returning from Boortree House until later that evening. He decided he must try to find out more about what lay behind Mrs Smith's distress.

CHAPTER 15
Small Talk at Boortree House

MACKENZIE WAS LISTENING to Primrose rehearse his great success in the Session; a subject which seemed to engross him more powerfully than the death of his client. He couldn't help but notice Primrose's fine attire: immaculate periwig, finely cut velvet jacket, silk handkerchief embroidered with his family crest – a ship – protruding from a pocket, expensive pair of shoes. His voice sounded refined, with less of a Scottish brogue than most other advocates. He was now describing some of the actual phrases he had used in Sir Lachlan's case. Like most ambitious men, thought MacKenzie, Primrose was a bore. He started looking for an excuse to end their conversation.

The huge room was full of chatter and laughter. Generous quantities of wine had removed the inhibitions of the guests. Suddenly a servant knocked into his companion and the contents of his wine glass splashed over his jacket. 'Fool!' shouted Primrose, hastily withdrawing his white handkerchief and scrubbing at the stain.

The peacock's feathers are ruffled! thought MacKenzie, just as he spotted Sir Lachlan's son across the room and thankfully made his excuses.

Hector gave him his hand.

'John, I am glad of the opportunity to speak with you. I was undecided whether to attend the celebration today since so little time has elapsed since the death of my father, but my sister persuaded me we should escape from brooding in Smith's chambers. I also hoped some of my father's friends would be here. There are many legal issues to be discussed before I can gain full possession of Glenshieldaig. I expect you have received my letter sanctioning your authority to investigate my father's death on behalf of the kin?'

'Yes, I will give the matter my full attention, Hector. But perhaps a party of this kind is not the place to discuss the details of inheritance law. I must arrange a suitable time when we can deal with your concerns in full.'

'You are right, please forgive me. My mind is driving me on too hard these days.'

'It is only natural. Your father has not yet been buried. Have all the plans for the funeral been made?'

'My kinsmen arrive today and we leave with my father's body tomorrow. Is there any word from Mr Stirling about his investigations?'

'Mr Stirling and his men continue to make enquiries.'

MacKenzie observed the young chief carefully. He was in many ways a smaller version of his father but more serious and without the chief's caustic wit.

'Some of my clansmen are convinced of Glenbeg's guilt and are ready to launch a feud against his clan and lay waste to the lands he once held,' Hector remarked. 'I have contained them so far, but the longer he remains in hiding, the more difficult it will be to restrain them from taking revenge against the Campbells. You know yourself how easily feuds can start and how difficult they are to stop. I pray it does not come to that, for I am of the strong opinion that violence between families should be consigned to the past. Feuds only hinder the work of sound estate management.'

'Wise words indeed, Hector. If only more of our fellow

Highlanders followed your example. Now, if you do not mind, I have a question or two to ask myself. Firstly, what do you make of George Scott? He appears to be an excellent match for your sister.'

'Ah! My sister has inherited the character of my father – there is no compromise with her – everything is black or white; she sees no middle road where people of different opinions can come to an accommodation. I may have to relent and allow her to marry Scott although, as you know, he brings little interest or money to the table. But he does hope to be an independent man and seeks service in the Army. My sister will be happier in foreign lands than in the Highlands.'

'And what of you, Hector. You are now free to marry the wife of your choice and pursue the policies you recommended to your father for so many years.'

The young chief hesitated before answering, aware that MacKenzie was framing his questions in a way he might do in a court of law.

'I must make a careful match, John. If I go to London and marry the daughter of an English nobleman and come back north with a fair tocher of £5,000 sterling, the family's financial position will be eased considerably. However, this will not be popular with my clan, who still hope I will marry the daughter of a chief. But that will only bring a few pennies to our empty bowl, since our neighbours are as bankrupt as ourselves. I cannot please everyone and now I must learn that compromises are necessary if I am to follow good policy. All I can say is that there will be changes at Glenshieldaig – my kinsmen know there have to be. The estate will be made more productive and I will cut the cost of my household. By removing one or two of our bards and musicians, who hold land for free, and by raising the rents of the tenants by a small degree, our finances could be in balance this year and the estate placed on a more secure footing. No new hangings will adorn the walls nor French furniture grace the chambers of Glenshieldaig Castle over the coming years. We must learn from the Dutch and English landowners. We cannot stand still or turn back the tide as my father hoped could be done. The world changes before our eyes – the old ways disappear like spring snow on a dyke.'

'I have heard reports you are considering a marriage to John Smith's daughter?'

'That is true. Smith was pushing for such a match but my father was against it. He believed the merchant class to be beneath us. I do not hold to this view. If Smith can make a good enough offer I will consider his daughter, but only if it benefits the House of Glenshieldaig.'

MacKenzie took a sip of wine.

'Mr Primrose has drawn up a list of creditors who were at law against your father. It includes a name I have never heard before, a surprise, I confess. As one of your father's advisers I was deeply involved in much of his legal work. The man concerned is James Sovrack. Do you know who he is?'

'I have never heard the name before, John. But my father could smell out a moneylender – there were always some willing to lend to him at usurious rates. Does Mr Primrose not know who the man is?'

'I have just spoken with him and he too is in the dark.'

'My father had travelled widely – he was well known in London, and even in Paris and Amsterdam. Perhaps the man belongs to one of these cities, for I know their streets crawl with those who make a living from lending money.'

'Yes, perhaps he is a foreign merchant. Anyway, I will have Mr Scougall take a careful look at the papers in Smith's house. If we can locate copies of the bonds to Sovrack, we will know who witnessed them and the date and place of signing.'

'I fear that will not be possible. The documents my father had with him in Edinburgh were sent back to the Highlands today. You may have to wait until you reach Glenshieldaig to gain further information about this man.'

'How inconvenient,' MacKenzie observed.

Hector MacLean did not reply but nodded his head slightly and looked round the room nervously. MacKenzie could see the young chief wanted to end their conversation, so he excused himself and, having thanked the Earl of Boortree for his hospitality, departed from the house.

CHAPTER 16

A Meeting with the Lord Advocate

ARCHIBALD STIRLING ALWAYS dreaded his interviews with the Lord Advocate. It was not that the Advocate possessed a particularly domineering tone or thunderous voice, but the fact that he himself was always on the defensive. He regretted accepting the position of Crown Officer – he should have continued with his work as an advocate, at which he was quite proficient. His wife had advised him to refuse the new position, but he had ignored her. She was proved correct, as usual. The temptation of something new, something different from the usual drudgery of court work had been too strong; that and his vanity. He had pictured himself as the associate of MacKenzie of Rosehaugh, author of *Aretina*, *Religio Stoici* and the great *Defence of the Antiquity of the Royal Line of Scotland*, with real power and influence for the first time in his life. However, he had not expected his new job to be so demanding and the great Rosehaugh had turned out to be more of a politician than a man of letters. Most of those who committed crime escaped and the blame came to rest, again and again, on his shoulders. And there was less and less time for his historical studies.

Stirling sat on a hard wooden chair in front of a vast desk which through age had taken on a black hue. The desk was very tidy with only two neat piles of paper on the left and right. He recalled the heaps of documents that were eternally accumulating in his small office across the corridor. The Advocate's efficiency was another thing which troubled him. He was a scrupulous manager of men and paper.

The Crown Officer gazed round the depressing room. There was little direct sunlight, only one small window near the ceiling; the chamber was lit by candles attached to the walls. He preferred more light and fresh air. There was a stale, putrid smell in here. Rosehaugh conducted interviews with prisoners in this very room – mostly of a political nature and thankfully outside the sphere of his responsibility. But it was well known that torture had been used on a number of occasions to elicit confessions. The thought of the thumbscrews made him shudder. The excruciating pain as the thumb was crushed to pulp. The leaders of the conventiclers had been dealt with very harshly. But what was to be done? As a student of the manoeuvrings of the 1640s, he knew well that Scottish politics was a brutal and dirty business. The security of the government was at stake. These men wanted to bring about a revolution in the church and state. At least he need not concern himself with such affairs. Perhaps King James would prove a more tolerant monarch than his elder brother.

On the walls were portraits of previous Lord Advocates. Their eyes seemed to stare accusingly at him, as if they knew he was not as committed as he should be to his work as Crown Officer. All appeared to be dour-faced figures who had devoted every moment of their existence to the law, so reaching the pinnacle of their profession. He could not fully understand such men. All he wanted was some peace to spend more time with his wife and daughters, and the other great passion of his life – his history of the Great Rebellion. Again a feeling of regret washed through him, mixed with despair; life was slipping away and nothing achieved.

The door opened and the Advocate, wearing a black gown and a long periwig, made straight for his seat without saying a word. His dress was indistinguishable from any other lawyer; black breeches and jacket. He carried some documents which he placed on his desk, and began to read from the one on top. At last he looked up; he was in his mid-fifties, with small darting eyes and a deathly white pallor. He was clearly suffering from a serious illness. There was a calm but determined look on his face as he spoke.

'Mr Stirling, I have read your report. There seems to be no conclusion to this affair. Or have you learnt anything further in the last few hours?'

'I have nothing more to report, sir. Glenbeg has still to be apprehended and I have discovered little more about the murders.'

'I am sure you are aware that the Privy Council wish this matter to be resolved with all haste. The Town Council are also voicing their concerns. Events of this kind sour the atmosphere of a town and are bad for trade. I have assured them both that you and your men are working night and day to find the killer. Am I correct in my assumption?'

The Advocate spoke quietly, his eyes moved from one side of the room to the other, as if following the flight of a swooping bird of prey, but did not meet the gaze of the Crown Officer. Stirling felt most uncomfortable. He could not say that he had been working night and day, but he had at least given the case his complete attention during office hours. Was he to devote his entire life to the pursuit of criminals?

'My Lordship, as you well know, for I have brought this matter to your attention on many occasions, I have only two men under me. Insufficient funds were made available and I was unable to attract the most suitable candidates. Innes is almost as old as I am; Miller, I am sure, is looking for a more highly paid position elsewhere, and as a result applies himself little. They do as they are told, but I fear they show scant initiative in their work.'

'Then you must manage them more carefully, Mr Stirling. If you are successful in apprehending the killer, or killers, of Sir Lachlan and Jossie I am sure I can persuade the Privy Council to grant your office a higher allowance. But at the moment you must make do with what you have and grind the millstone a little harder.'

Rosehaugh placed a harsh emphasis on his last words. There was anger in his voice.

Stirling saw the corner of the Advocate's mouth twitch. In his mind he heard the screams as Rosehaugh ordered the thumbscrews to be tightened. Did he ever show any emotion? There was no nobility in servants of the state any more.

'I will do my best, sir.'

'Your report informs me that Sir Lachlan's kinsmen have arrived to escort his body to Glenshieldaig. May I recommend that you do the family the honour of attending his funeral. It is possible you may uncover information critical to the case from such a journey. Leave one of your men here. I will supervise the tasks you set him.'

Stirling was dismayed to hear Rosehaugh's order. He had not intended to travel to Glenshieldaig. It was not the thought of the Highlands that depressed him, but the miserable inns lining the route, so-called Highland hospitality. He would be away from home for a full week at least, or more. His wife would not be pleased. He would have to postpone his studies again. Why was his real work frustrated at every turn?

CHAPTER 17
A Cup of Ale in the Canongate

IT WAS DARK when Scougall emerged from St Giles Kirk and headed down the High Street in the direction of Holyroodhouse. Against his natural inclinations he had decided to act decisively. Surely he had been directed to St Giles for a reason: so that he might witness the distress of Smith's wife. It was now his responsibility to find out as much as he could about what was happening in the household. He would show MacKenzie that he was not just a dull scribe. Armed with new determination he marched confidently through the Netherbow Port and into the Canongate, where the tenements were not so high and there were fewer shops and taverns.

However, as he approached his destination, he became less confident. His pace slowed, until he found himself standing at the threshold of the merchant's house without the nerve to knock on the door. What was he to say to Mr Smith? He was not an advocate like MacKenzie; he had never stood up in a court room and vigorously questioned an accused. He could not remember vigorously questioning anyone, except perhaps his young sisters, and that was many years ago. What possible reason could he give for such a call? He was not a close friend of the family, having only met Smith on one occasion, and had never spoken to his wife. He was gripped by intense anxiety and his face flushed at the thought of the pitiful image of a tongue-tied fool he would present if the door was answered.

His paroxysm of self-doubt was interrupted abruptly by the arrival of Smith's maidservant Peggy, carrying a wicker basket filled with fresh fruit and vegetables.

'Mr Scougall, sir. Are ye callin on ma maister an mistress?'

Scougall was put on the defensive for he had not noticed Peggy approaching.

'No... well, yes. I was wishing to see... Mr Smith,' he spluttered.

'Well, in ye come, Mr Scougall. I'm afraid they are baith out at the moment. But Mr Smith will be back shortly. Ye can wait in ma maister's chamber.'

Scougall was lost for words. All he could think of doing was to follow Peggy into the house. As he climbed the stairs behind her to the first floor where Smith lived with his family, he could not help but notice the swagger of her hips moving from side to side. He remembered the look she had given Mr Hope on the night Sir Lachlan was killed. What could this sonsie girl see in a fat old minister? Scougall found himself admiring the view as he ascended the stairs behind her. But he suddenly recalled that he had just been in St Giles asking God to deliver him from sin! He tried to think about something else.

Peggy opened the door with her key. Scougall was reminded of the room in which they had been entertained by Sir Lachlan – it was the same size and furnished in similar fashion: a large oak table, a long wooden sideboard, a few chairs and portraits on the walls. But instead of Scottish monarchs, the paintings were of the Smith family. Scougall recognised one of the merchant himself.

'Please be seated,' said Peggy with a smile.

Scougall sat down on one of the fine upholstered chairs.

What was he to talk about until Smith returned, and then what was he to say?

'Would ye care for onything tae drink, Mr Scougall?'

Scougall was not thirsty but he heard himself say, 'A little ale would suffice, thank you.'

Peggy disappeared to fetch the drink. He thought of his master when they had visited Hope. He must act in a similar manner. MacKenzie would make the most of such an opportunity. He must have confidence – he had been shown a sign in St Giles.

Peggy soon returned with a pewter tankard of ale. His eyes could not fail to catch her ample cleavage as she bent over to place the beer on a small table beside him. Her face was not pretty but there was something about her.

'Now, Mr Scougall, are ye happy to wait until Mr Smith returns? I've some work to be gettin on wi.'

'Peggy,' began Scougall, summoning up the courage to ask what for him was a very forward question, 'has Mrs Smith been greatly upset by the death of Sir Lachlan?'

'She's been upset about the scandal, sir. I don't think she was too sorry tae see Sir Lachlan depairt himsel – she thought he was a bit o a burden, for he was never payin Mr Smith onything.'

'I see,' said Scougall. 'I only ask because earlier this evening I saw her in St Giles and she was weeping.' Usually Scougall would not have discussed such information with a servant, but he sensed that sharing this with Peggy might reap rewards, and he was not disappointed.

Peggy appeared excited to hear such news. She lowered her voice and an earnest expression spread over her face.

'Is that right? I hae never seen ma mistress sheddin tears afore. But there's been some mighty strange affairs in this hoose oer the last few days.'

'What in particular?' asked Scougall, trying not to appear too interested.

'Well, first of aw that business wi Sir Lachlan. And now there's mair trouble, I'm no sure what. These walls are thick and ma maister and mistress keep things tae themselves, but I ken when something's wrang and I ken this much aboot what caused it. A letter arrived this mornin. I'm sure it was frae yon strange creature Glenbeg, I heard his name mentioned and it was posted in Perth – I spoke wi the man who delivered it. There were long talks between Mr and Mrs Smith aw mornin. I kenned somethin was happenin, for ma maister left unexpectedly and said he would no return till later this evening. Ma mistress said she intended to visit her sister in Gray's Wynd. I ken weel that Glenbeg is suspected o killin Sir Lachlan and that he's ran off; and now I'm wondrin what else he's done. Maybe I've said too much, Mr Scougall, I find ye an easy man tae talk wi.'

She gave the young notary her most alluring stare.

Scougall's thoughts, however, were now focused elsewhere. He was delighted with what he had gleaned.

'Was Glenbeg a friend of Mr Smith?'

'He was seen roond here now and again, but I was feart o him. That face! The haunds o a skeleton! Braith like a reekin corpse! I think ma maister had lent him money – what ither reason would draw a fiend like Glenbeg here?'

'Do you know where Mr Smith has gone?'

'He didnae tell me but I guessed frae his face that he was attendin tae important business. I'm sure it was about Glenbeg. I've heard it told that he has killed afore...'

Peggy suddenly dried up in mid flow, aware that the consequences of passing on the fruit of her eavesdropping could be severe. The Smiths were a good family to work for and she did not want to lose her position. She had already risked much with that stupid minister who had promised to give her a few of his recipes. 'Now, ye must excuse me sir.'

Scougall sought to change the subject: 'How old are you Peggy?'

'I will be fifteen in July,' she said, returning his smile as she left the room.

Scougall sat alone, staring at Mr Smith's fine clock which stood on the mantelpiece. Time drifted by. He had arrived at seven o'clock and it was now five minutes to eight. He could not sit here all night watching the clock, he told himself, he had to pack for tomorrow's journey.

At last he shouted through to Peggy and excused himself, asking her to inform Mr Smith that he had called and would visit again on his return from the Highlands. Before Peggy reappeared to warn him about the dangers of his destination, he had shown himself out.

As Scougall walked back up the High Street towards his lodgings he passed a small figure hurrying down in the opposite direction. Mr Smith had a look of anguish on his face. The merchant did not see the young lawyer.

CHAPTER 18
A Letter for Davie Scougall

WHEN SCOUGALL RETURNED to Foster's Wynd he hoped to make straight for his chamber. He opened the door as quietly as he could for he did not want to disturb Mrs Baird, the relict of Mr Baird, merchant, from whom he rented his room. He was just about to place a foot on the first step of the stair when he heard her calling.

'Mr Davie, do ye no want onything tae eat this evening?'

'No thank you, Mrs Baird. I have had a long day and wish to retire to my bed early.'

Mrs Baird, an old woman in her seventies, dressed plainly in black, appeared through a doorway. She was so diminutive that Scougall towered over her.

She may be old but she has the ears of a fox, he thought.

'How mony times have I telt ye no tae work sae hard. Look at my dear Willie – workin every day o his life frae the age o fourteen tae the day he died at only fifty, leaving me a poor relict these six and twenty years. Find time for leisure, Mr Davie.'

Scougall had heard her saying this many times before and he always gave the same reply: 'I play golf, Mrs Baird.' She did not seem to regard golf as recreation.

'Good night,' he said firmly. 'I'll not be at breakfast tomorrow. I rise early to watch the Highlanders take Sir

Lachlan's coffin. Then I travel in the company of Mr MacKenzie to attend the chief's burial.'

The old woman shook her head, looking as if someone had just told her about a death in her family.

'The Hielands! Whatever is Mr MacKenzie doing sending a poor boy off tae sic a place.' Scougall was about to ascend the stairs when she continued, 'I almost forgot, this letter came for ye in the early evening. It was delivered by Mr MacKenzie's servant.'

Scougall came back down the stairs to collect it.

The arrival of a letter was a rare occasion. His mother wrote perhaps once every few months and his sisters the odd letter. MacKenzie must be sending him some final instructions about the journey.

Mrs Baird at last retreated to her fireside and he was able to escape to his small room on the first floor. The window faced south, overlooking the gardens which lay behind the close. The room was simply furnished with a bed and table but it was cosy, as Mrs Baird had lit a small fire earlier. A set of golf clubs leaned on the wall in one corner. Scougall's copy of Blair took pride of place on the cabinet by his bed. He recalled the gently mocking words of MacKenzie when he had introduced him to Sir Lachlan in the Periwig:

'Davie is one of the fortunate disciples of our learned friend Mr Hugh Blair, author of that most loquacious of legal tomes, and considered by some poor souls, as the notary's Bible, *The Art and Style of the Scottish Writer*.'

A few other books, mostly theological and legal texts, had been placed carefully on the table where Scougall seated himself and, having lit a candle, broke the seal of red wax and opened the letter.

He did not recognise the hand.

It was not from his master.

Libberton's Wynd
16 May 1686

Dear Mr Scougall,

Just a short note to inform you of my findings
today. I met with my friends Jean Guthrie and
Margaret Oliphant for we had arranged to visit some
of Edinburgh's shops. All the talk, as you can imagine,
was of Sir Lachlan and Mr Jossie and my friends were
intrigued to learn that my father and you were on the
killer's or killers' trail. I hope you are not offended,
but I turned our conversation towards jewellery saying
that I admired a particular brooch I had seen – the
brooch you described to me. Good news, Mr Scougall!
Miss Oliphant has seen the very same in John Nisbet's
shop in Bell's Wynd. We were most excited by this
discovery and at once made for his shop, where we
found a range of such brooches in different sizes being
sold at a reduced price of 5 shillings – the jeweller
bemoaned the fact that they had not sold well. He
remembers only two being bought: one by a soldier,
a young man in his twenties – he does not know his
name – and the other by an elderly woman.

I hope this information proves useful.

Your affectionate friend,
Elizabeth MacKenzie

Scougall read the letter over again in rising excitement. The
details about the brooch invigorated him; even more so, that
it was from Elizabeth. He must write a reply immediately and
send it tomorrow morning. He rummaged around until he had
found a sheet of paper and began to write with his quill.

CHAPTER 19
Sir Lachlan's Funeral Cortège

AN HOUR AFTER sunrise, around two hundred men and women had gathered in the Canongate outside the house of John Smith. Scougall and MacKenzie stood near the front door, trying to keep warm by stamping their feet on the ground. Behind them was a gallimaufry of onlookers – lawyers, merchants, servants, artisans and a rabble of beggars hoping to profit from the munificence of the young chief, for it was the custom that the poor were to be provided for at such times. In the crowd were some who had known the deceased and others who had never heard of him until his untimely death. However, they had all risen early to witness the spectacle of the clansmen of Sir Lachlan, the nobility of a Highland clan, the MacLeans of Glenshieldaig, collecting the body of their dead chief to escort him back to the clan lands for burial.

The crowd was silent, mesmerised by the sight of thirty mounted Highlanders in tartan plaids of different colours, which gave them the look of another world against the plain blacks and browns of the citizens of Edinburgh. Each clansmen had a leather targe flung over his back and a long broadsword hanging by his side.

Hector MacLean and his sister emerged from the doorway, both dressed in Lowland clothing. They acknowledged MacKenzie and Scougall and other friends. Then the coffin appeared behind them, carried by six tartan-clad men, and was placed on a simple wooden cart. Coins were distributed to the city's poor by Hector's men. Hector himself, his sister and the coffin-bearers mounted their horses and led the strange party up the High Street towards the Netherbow Port and then turned right onto Leith Wynd.

When the cortège had disappeared, Mr Primrose emerged from the throng and came over to greet MacKenzie and Scougall.

'Gentlemen, may I have a few words?'

'Of course, Mr Primrose,' said MacKenzie.

'I have been very busy with work these last few days – I wanted to ask you about Jossie's murder. It is rumoured that he met his end by the same hand as Sir Lachlan. Have you heard anything about Stirling's enquiries?'

'I fear he has left most stones unturned and the ones he has turned have revealed little,' said MacKenzie in a serious tone. 'Davie and I, at the request of the kin, have been examining the evidence in an attempt to determine the identity of the person behind our good friend's death.'

'And what have you discovered?' Primrose asked eagerly.

'Let us say that progress is being made.'

'I fear,' said Primrose, 'that Glenbeg killed Sir Lachlan in a debauched fit. It is well known he is a man of unstable character and I have heard it said he is wanted for the murder of a soldier in the United Provinces.'

Scougall was disturbed to hear this allegation against Glenbeg again. From Peggy's mouth it had seemed more like sensational gossip. As a statement by an advocate it was a different matter. He shivered to reflect that he had sat in such company at Sir Lachlan's table. Robert Campbell had barely spoken during the meal, despite having consumed a substantial quantity of wine. He remembered him looking intently at his cards as if the answer to the mysteries of the universe were to be found there.

'I have heard a version of this many times before, Mr Primrose, and it is different at each telling,' smiled MacKenzie.

'It is perhaps an old wives' tale,' Primrose responded, 'but there may be some truth in it. Now, gentlemen, you must excuse me. I leave for Culross, where I must attend to family affairs – I'll make my way to Glenshieldaig from there. I understand that you also travel to the Highlands. I bid you safe journey.'

The crowd had now dispersed and only a few figures remained on the street. John Smith and his wife stood at their front door, looking pale and distraught, talking to Mr Hope.

Scougall was eager for an opportunity to tell MacKenzie of his discoveries of the previous evening but Stirling now approached. He was looking worried.

'My Lord Advocate has spoken with me about the murders and is not well pleased with the little I have discovered so far, John,' he announced. 'He has political concerns at the moment, fearing his enemies may oust him from his position. I have sent my men to Jossie's shop to examine the scene of the second crime but I must admit I am baffled. Have you or Mr Scougall had any further ideas?'

'Davie and I continue to grapple with the facts – we now have official sanction from the kin of Sir Lachlan. The other night we went to the shop, where we disturbed an intruder who knocked Davie to the ground on trying to escape. We chased the fellow, but he was too fast for us and we lost him on the High Street. When we returned to the shop, I made a thorough examination and discovered two things – the last four pages of Jossie's ledger had been torn out, and this small brooch, which was lying on the floor.'

MacKenzie removed the brooch from his pocket and gave

it to the Crown Officer.

'It should remain in your hands, Archibald. It may have been dropped by Jossie's assailant, or it may have been lying on the floor for weeks. Mr Jossie did not keep a clean shop. I intend to engage in further research this morning. Then Mr Scougall and I leave for the Highlands to attend Sir Lachlan's funeral. I feel confident we will learn more at Glenshieldaig. I will keep in contact, if I may, by post, and inform you of anything pertinent I learn.'

Stirling told them he was also travelling to the Highlands and that he would make his way in the company of Mr Hope and Mr Primrose once the latter's business in Culross was concluded.

The Crown Officer then turned to Scougall and smiled.

'Is this your first journey to the Highlands? I do hope you will be well armed.' He waited for a troubled look to appear on the young notary's face before continuing, 'Do not worry Mr Scougall – I only jest with you. I have spent many a fine week fishing and hunting on the lands of Campbell of Glenmore – Sir Colin Campbell was a client of mine. You may be surprised by what you find. I even took a few words of Gaelic back with me.'

MacKenzie and Stirling laughed but Scougall did not see the joke.

'It was the policy of our good King James to extirpate the barbaric tongue and I must concur with him,' he expostulated. 'Education of the Highlander in good Scots would certainly hasten the progress of civilisation there!'

'Come, Davie, you still have much to learn despite the progress you have made in the law. I look forward to revealing a different picture to the one etched deep by Presbyterian divines and your grandmother's fireside tales.'

When Stirling departed Scougall did not let the opportunity

slip. MacKenzie listened attentively as he described his walk down Steel's Close, his discovery of bloodstains, witnessing Mrs Smith's distress in St Giles and his interview with Peggy.

'And my evening ended as Mr Smith passed me on the High Street with a very worried expression on his face.'

'Well done, I am glad you have been so busy,' replied MacKenzie. 'The Smith household would appear to be in a state of some distress. It's unclear whether this is the effect of Sir Lachlan's death or if there is some deeper cause. As I have said, we must keep Mr Smith and his wife in our thoughts.'

MacKenzie was impressed by Scougall's efforts. He was showing considerable initiative.

'I also have another confession to make, sir, and I do not know if you will be well pleased with me,' Scougall went on. 'At breakfast yesterday I mentioned to your daughter that you had found a brooch in Jossie's shop and I described it to her. Last night I received a short note from her informing me that a jeweller by the name of John Nisbet in Bell's Wynd stocks similar brooches and is selling them at a price of five shillings.'

It was as though a sheet of glass had fallen through MacKenzie's joviality.

'It would appear you have made something of an impression on my daughter. Davie, I must advise you in future not to pass on information that I have shared with you in confidence to any others, not even to Elizabeth, nor to Stirling and his men. For when we let loose a minnow, a dogfish may return to bite us!'

Scougall was wounded by MacKenzie's rebuke. It was the first time he had displeased his new master and he felt shamed. He realised that he must tread more carefully as far as Elizabeth was concerned.

But MacKenzie's good humour soon returned and he

continued in a more conciliatory tone, 'What I mean, Davie, is that we must be careful that the evidence we have collected does not find its way into the hands of Sir Lachlan's killer. It may prove vital if we are to have the murderer prosecuted. So I recommend caution. A lawyer must know when to hold his peace and when to speak out. But do not look so worried – you have the eagerness of youth. I will write to Elizabeth tonight, requesting some more details and advising caution, for we are fishers in drumlie water. Now you must show me these bloodstains before we leave.'

CHAPTER 20
Queensferry

THE TWO LAWYERS stood on the shore; MacKenzie gazed northwards across the water, enjoying the cool breeze on his face, watching the shadows of clouds move briskly over the hills. Scougall stared down at the pebbles beneath his feet and kicked some into the water. He picked up a flat stone which caught his eye and sent it skimming over the surface of the grey, counting seven times before it disappeared into the sea.

'You throw a fine skimmer,' said MacKenzie and smiled to himself. He had taken to his young assistant. There was something endearing about his lack of pretension. He had tenacious qualities and much promise. His views were certainly rough hewn and some stood in direct opposition to sound reason, but he would be influenced by a little philosophy. MacKenzie realised that he enjoyed his company very much. He wondered if this was what a father felt towards a son. The image of his own sons came to him, stillborn twins in their tiny coffins. How desolate life could be. But there was still goodness in this bleak world. When he was engaged with in an intriguing case like this one, the pit lay in the distance and his mind danced in the light.

Scougall picked up another stone and this time threw it as high as he could. It seemed to hang for a few seconds in the blue, before it fell against grey cloud, disappeared, and plopped onto the surface of a wave.

'It's here at last!' MacKenzie pointed to the small boat heading towards them. 'Now our journey can begin.'

The ferry arrived at the small quay within minutes and, once three merchants had disembarked, the two lawyers boarded. MacKenzie paid the ferryman and they took their places on a wooden bench.

'Now, Davie, let me share some of the latest information I have unearthed. Yesterday I met George Scott at Boortree House. He struck me as a serious young man. He is determined to marry Ann MacLean. I then spoke with my kinsman Kenneth Chisholm, who supplied me with some interesting details about his family. George is a younger son of Sir David Scott of Drumsheugh – a landowner of some substance in the south-west, who was strong for the king in the civil wars. Their story is similar to many families of that time. Sir David was an enterprising man who had many ideas about how to increase the produce of his lands. But all his projects, like so many of that ilk, returned little or nothing. His business ventures were ended by the disruptions following the signing of the National Covenant in 1638. A staunch supporter of the king, he had been awarded a monopoly of pearl fishing in his local rivers by King Charles' father, our good King James, and even though the rivers provided but a handful of pearls over twenty years, the dignity Sir David attached to his gift encouraged his loyalty to the monarch.'

MacKenzie, who until then had been staring back in the direction of Edinburgh, turned his gaze on his young friend. Scougall was not looking his usual self. He had taken on a greyish pallor so that it seemed the grey water of the firth was reflected on his face.

'Are you feeling unwell, Davie?' asked MacKenzie.

'I fear I am ill as a result of the motion of this boat, sir. But please continue with your history of the House of Drumsheugh, so that I may be distracted from this terrible nausea.'

MacKenzie promptly obliged.

'Sir David was strong for King Charles, as I have said, and he and his eldest sons fought with Montrose in that grim series of battles between the King and the Covenanters in the 1640s. I have read a number of accounts of these tragic encounters and spoken to a few of those, including Sir Lachlan himself, who fought and survived them. It was a time when the veins of our country were opened and much blood spilt. A close scrutiny of the causes of this war would prove a useful exercise, Davie. Archibald Stirling might provide you with a list of sources. As I think I mentioned, he is an enthusiastic student of the period.'

Scougall groaned. MacKenzie took that as a cue to continue his narrative.

'Sir David's eldest son was slain at the Battle of Kilsyth and two others died at Philiphaugh. Years in exile on the Continent followed. George Scott, the youngest of the family, was not born until 1654. At the Restoration the family recovered their estates but the lands had been ravaged in the '40s and ill-managed since. They still labour to this day to improve their rents. Like Sir Lachlan, Drumsheugh was caught in a web of debt. The surviving sons were scattered to the four winds to make their fortunes outside Scotland. George returned to Europe and pursued a career as a soldier of fortune, fighting for any government that would pay his fee. He eventually came back to our shores last year after many adventures, and met Ann MacLean in Edinburgh. It seems that on one occasion Sir Lachlan threatened George in public that his life was in danger if he continued to see his daughter.'

MacKenzie stopped talking as Scougall made a choking sound, flung himself round and retched violently into the waters of the firth. MacKenzie moved over beside him and patted his back.

'There, Davie, you'll feel better now. Luckily we'll be striking dry land in a few minutes!'

Scougall continued to groan as he lay on the bench on his stomach, his mouth over the edge of the boat in case he vomited again. Cold sea water splashed onto his face, providing some relief.

They soon reached the Fife shore and MacKenzie helped him off the ferry. Scougall staggered up the path towards the old inn, where horses were for hire. He found a grassy verge, lay down flat on his back and closed his eyes. MacKenzie, laughing loudly, sat down beside him.

'You told me your uncle was a seaman. There is little sea blood in your veins!'

'I have never been one for water, sir. I cannot swim and that was the first journey on a boat I have ever made. I hope it will be my last.'

'Then I think we may be forced to return by another route, Davie.'

Scougall was lying on a bank surrounded by wild flowers, resting his head on the palms of his hands and staring up at the clouds drifting across the blue. He remained in this position for a few minutes, thanking God he had decided to follow the profession of notary and not become a merchant plying the Baltic trade as had been discussed in the family – a dry office was preferable any day.

'I'm beginning to feel myself again, sir. You were telling me of Sir Lachlan's threat. Both George or Ann MacLean, or both of them, might have wanted rid of him to marry at leisure.'

MacKenzie was lost in horticultural thoughts, admiring the architectural magnificence of the tiny bluebell and noticing a decaying primrose flower beside Scougall's head.

'Yes, Davie,' he murmured.

'I was convinced that Ann MacLean was involved from the start...'

'Perhaps, Davie,' interrupted MacKenzie, recollecting himself, 'but as yet we have no proof. And would it not have been easier for the two lovers to elope rather than commit such crimes? There were two other men present at Sir Lachlan's lodgings on the night of his death, to whom we have not as yet given our full attention – Mr Primrose and John Smith. They are of course upstanding citizens of Edinburgh, that goes without saying, and I do not wish to link their names unnecessarily with these heinous crimes, but we must examine their characters if we are to have a complete picture. You must never leave any stone unturned when you are concerned with murder; that is the lesson I have learned from my years as a lawyer. Smith is by all accounts an honest burgess, an elder of St Giles, a member of the burgh council and is well-liked by all I have spoken to. He is regarded as an astute man of business, who is generally fair and honest in his dealings. However, I have found two points of grievance between him and Sir Lachlan. The first we know already. He was owed considerable sums of money and had only seen small amounts paid back. I have also talked with Smith's servant girl Peggy. After some encouragement she readily confessed to her liaison with the good Mr Hope. She also informed me that on a number of occasions she had heard Smith and Sir Lachlan discussing a possible marriage between Hector and Smith's daughter Jean. As we might expect, Sir Lachlan was steadfast against such a match on the grounds that he considered a merchant, even a rich one, to be far beneath his position in society. Smith apparently applied pressure, threatening to take the chief through the courts to recover his debts but Sir Lachlan could not be persuaded. Peggy told me it was the only time that she has ever heard her master lose his temper.'

'But would such a matter drive Mr Smith to the desperate act of murder?' asked Scougall, whose natural colour was beginning to return. 'And did Smith and his wife not witness a figure ascending the stairs after we had left the lodgings on the night of Sir Lachlan's murder?'

'Regarding your first point, Davie, I agree it seems unlikely that a man of Smith's exemplary character would be driven to such extreme action. There are, after all, wealthier matches for his daughter. And Sir Lachlan, even though he was a friend of many years' standing, was not always easy and obliging. But on your second point, many a wife has lied for her husband. We must not rule him out of our thoughts entirely. Now, here are our horses. At least some colour has returned to your cheeks. We must travel with speed if we are to make Perth by nightfall.'

They made their way up a muddy track heading north through the fields of Fife. The day was still fine and apart from a couple of chapmen heading south to Edinburgh they had the road to themselves.

CHAPTER 21
A Highland Tryst

A SMALL FIRE burned beside a Highland burn. The sky was steel grey and on both sides of the glen sheer slopes rose to high mountains. A long black ridge was visible to the west and the eastern peaks were encased in snow. A rudimentary path snaked northwards to disappear in the mist about a mile away. The wind was blowing strongly and sleet had begun to fall. Around the flickering flames were five hunched figures, dressed in dark plaids and old bonnets, their filthy, bearded faces suggested they spent most of their lives in the open.

Each man was concentrating on the task at hand: consuming an evening meal, for a sheep had recently been slaughtered and roasted on the fire. The remains of its carcass lay a few feet away from where they ate. The men did not speak to each other. It had been days since their last proper meal and it was their intention to devour as much as they could. They did not know when they might enjoy such a feast again.

A sudden noise in the distance disturbed their lonely repast. One of them stood up to get a better view as a rider appeared over a small knoll a couple of hundred yards to the south. The rest remained seated and only raised their eyes. The knives they were using to slice off pieces of meat flashed in the firelight.

The sun dipped below the western ridge and the glen

darkened. When the horseman reached the fire, he dismounted and uttered a greeting in Gaelic. He was wearing the same dismal attire, but unlike his comrades was beardless. On his neck a long scar was visible, curving from his gullet up to his chin and round onto his cheek. He was handed a lump of greasy mutton, which he began to eat ravenously, the juices dripping from his toothless mouth down his chin and onto his plaid.

It was a few minutes before he began to speak and by this time the others had filled their stomachs to the point where they could eat no more. He removed a small leather pouch from under his plaid and poured the contents onto the ground beside the fire. Long screams of exultation rose into the glen and were lost in the wind. The silver coins were picked up carefully, each one held tenderly and examined for authenticity. They were then placed in a small pile. The men stared at their prize for a few moments until the latecomer carefully divided up the spoils.

CHAPTER 22
A Few Words at Glenfarg

SCOUGALL AND MACKENZIE travelled on through the rolling countryside. After a few hours a large loch appeared on their right with hills rising from the far bank. In the middle of the water was an island, on which stood a ruined castle surrounded by trees.

'That was where Queen Mary was held captive after her deposition, Davie, and where she escaped from,' said MacKenzie.

'Then this is Loch Leven and those hills in the distance are the Lomond Hills,' answered Scougall, who was delighted to see this place, which he had heard so much about.

'Having escaped this prison, she found herself in another when she crossed the border into England – Queen Elizabeth was not welcoming,' said MacKenzie.

'But Mary would have reinstated the Papist religion in both Scotland and England.' Scougall was always happy to discuss one of his favourite topics in Scottish history.

'It has always amazed me, Davie, how human beings strive to divide themselves into different sects and how history, a subject which should educate us about the follies of the past, becomes another weapon in the wars of the present.'

Scougall was unsure how to answer and remained silent until they reached a small settlement.

'Where are we, sir?'

'This is Glenfarg, Davie. We will rest in the inn for a short while and take some refreshment.'

They dismounted and entered a two-storey dwelling house, which to Scougall's eyes looked little different from the rest of the squat buildings in the small township. Once inside, he realised they were in a hostelry of a most basic kind. A decrepit innkeeper indicated with a grunt that they should sit down at one of the tables. The place was dark, dirty and stinking.

'Now Davie, there are some other details I wish to share with you about the character and family history of Mr Primrose. You have already told me your impression of him – a fine lawyer with great prospects, perhaps prone to conceit. I disagree with none of this. He belongs to the family of Primrose of Culross, who have made their money over the last hundred years. His great-grandfather secured their fortune through trade with the Baltic in the time of King James; his grandfather advanced their wealth, becoming a moneylender to the nobility of King Charles and his father is still a man of substance, having preserved the family's money during the Wars of the Covenant by recalling loans at a small loss and selling others before the country fell into civil strife and the market for credit collapsed. Many others less astute were ruined. Younger sons of the family were encouraged to pursue careers in the law. Primrose's great-uncle became Clerk of the Privy Council and his uncle was a writer, like yourself, who gained the position of collector of fines from those in the Highlands who had protected the Clan Gregor. As a result he was very unpopular with that unlucky kindred, and with many other clans who had helped the MacGregors over the many years they were relentlessly pursued by the Campbells. Another uncle became an advocate and rose to the bench as Lord Dourobin. Some anticipate that Mr Primrose will eventually rise to become a judge like his uncle.'

MacKenzie stopped to take a sip from the tankard of ale that had been placed in front of him by the innkeeper.

'It is the history of every successful Scottish family since the Glorious Revolution of 1560 when our nation made its monumental break with Rome,' interjected Scougall.

'Yes, Davie,' said MacKenzie, cutting him off quickly, 'Now, let me continue. One of his great-uncles was passed over in the family succession. It was something of a scandal back in the '20s. Walter Primrose was accused and convicted of being a warlock and committing abominable acts on horses. He was sentenced to be strangled and burned at the stake on the Castle Hill of Edinburgh, but he escaped from the Tolbooth the night before he was to be executed and was never heard of again. Many thought he had escaped abroad – others that he had fled to live the life of a broken man in the Highlands. Ever since his disappearance, tales have been told in Culross about his return, especially when a stranger is seen in the town. At the time this was a great calumny for such an ambitious family and it took many years for these events to fade from people's memories – it perhaps accounts for their attempts ever since to play a very close political game. It may also explain the driving ambition of our Mr Primrose.'

'Madness often skips a generation,' Scougall said, delighted to hear that Primrose had some imperfection in his pedigree.

'We now have a fuller picture of most of the characters under our scrutiny, although relatively little of Smith's wife and daughter, who were both present in the house at the time of Sir Lachlan's death. Smith's own testimony states they remained in their chambers for the entire evening. Margaret Smith is the daughter of an East Lothian minister and known as a hard-working and devout woman. Her daughter is a girl of but twelve years. They were both interviewed by Stirling and their accounts do not differ from John Smith's. Although we do of course know that Mrs Smith attended St Giles Kirk last night in an anguished state. Come, Davie, let us drink up.'

MacKenzie left a few coins on the table and bid farewell to the innkeeper, who grunted an unintelligible reply. Once outside he stroked the back of his horse.

'It now only leaves you and me, Davie. And I have already said I believe you are incapable of committing such a crime. Am I correct in my supposition?' MacKenzie's eyes sparkled with mischief.

Scougall looked worried.

'I think you are, sir. I admit that my family has had its sorrows. I have mentioned my uncle's difficulties with drink and melancholia.'

'All families have such problems, Davie. I could entertain you for hours with stories of Highland madness. My clan in particular seems to be plagued with such an affliction. It is not a thing to be feared, it's all part of human nature. Nevertheless, there is one person we have not yet considered.'

'Who is that, sir?' asked Scougall.

'Consider this. It is quite possible that I could have returned to Sir Lachlan's lodgings, poisoned him and then killed the apothecary – quite possible. Mr Stirling has not made any detailed assessment of my whereabouts apart from our initial statements. Are you convinced I am innocent of the crime?'

Scougall was surprised by the direction the conversation was taking.

'I believe you played no part in these terrible events, sir.'

'And on what basis have you formed this opinion?'

'I just... know. I cannot prove it. It is of course possible you were responsible. I don't think you were... I know you weren't. You're a fine lawyer, a clerk of the Session, many clients have placed their trust in you, you're rich and successful and have a beautiful house and a… daughter,' Scougall stammered, turning red.

'Don't worry, Davie. I am not guilty – unless I was possessed by a spirit which laid a cloak over my consciousness. But in any investigation you must learn to keep an open mind and cover all eventualities. Almost anything is possible in this world; that is what I have learned from many years in our law courts. Good men can be driven to do bad deeds, evil men do good ones. Keep that in your mind and think about me. What is my story? Could it explain that I am the murderer?'

'I know enough to believe you are a good man. That is sufficient for me. I have faith in you as I have in God.'

'Come,' said MacKenzie as he mounted his horse, 'I will entertain you with the story of my life as we ride down to Perth.'

Scougall pulled himself into the saddle and they followed the track heading north out of the village. 'I will not bore you with a history of the MacKenzie clan. Genealogies can easily become tedious if they are not your own, and a full description of the exploits of my kin would last the whole journey to Glenshieldaig. But do remind me to give you a manuscript which is in my possession covering the early history. My father, Roderick MacKenzie, was given the lands of Ardcoul by his father, the famous Roderick MacKenzie tutor of Kintail – my mother was a Chisholm. I was the third son of their marriage and was fostered with a neighbouring family at the age of seven, a practice which was then common in the Highlands. It was a great wrench to be taken from my mother.'

MacKenzie was briefly lost in his own thoughts, remembering the ceremony that had taken place more than forty years before, when he had been presented to his foster parents: Gillecreist and Katherine MacKenzie. He had stood in his bedchamber in Ardcoul Castle, dressed in his finest shirt and breeches, while his mother, tears streaming down her cheeks, said her final goodbyes. At the time he had been too excited to think about missing her. He recalled riding proudly beside his father and kinsmen to the house of his foster parents, where a crowd was waiting for him – he had a wonderful feeling of importance, of being the centre of the world. He had stood silently, as instructed, listening to the old lawman sealing the contract in Gaelic, which was then laboriously translated into English and written down by his father's notary. That evening a great feast had been held in his honour, followed by music, songs and stories. It had been the stories, some told by bards, others by clansmen of his father, that had most exhilarated him. They painted pictures of distant times, of battles and adventure. He had always loved such tales. And then the next morning he remembered waking in a strange bedchamber; finding himself part of a new family which spoke not one word of English.

'I attended the burgh school of the Chanonry of Ross and at the age of fourteen was sent south to university at Aberdeen, where I spent four years before travelling to Leiden to study law. At first I hated Holland. I found it a dismal place after my student days in Scotland and the taste I had had of the joyous life of London on my way to the United Provinces. I detested the University of Leiden and was much affected by low spirits, but I made friends with my fellow students and a number of the Dutch and greatly enjoyed my travels in France and Italy after my legal studies.'

'I have always wished to travel abroad, sir,' said Scougall.

'And one day you shall, Davie. On my return to Scotland I became an advocate in the Court of Session and pursued a career in the law. I married the daughter of a Fife laird and we had a daughter. But my wife died in childbirth and the following years were a time of great sadness Davie – the worst of my life. I was struck hard by melancholy, which did not lift for a long time and still afflicts me. I seemed to live life as in a dream. But I finally emerged from the pit, pulled out by the soft words of my daughter as she grew into a beautiful child. There you have it Davie, the story of my life. Probe deeper if you may.'

Scougall was deeply moved by the personal details that MacKenzie had revealed to him and waited for a few minutes before posing a question.

'Did not the promise of your wife's eternal life provide you with some comfort during those dark days?'

MacKenzie stopped his horse and Scougall was forced to do likewise.

'No it did not,' he sighed. 'I have already told you I have little time for theology. By upbringing I am an Episcopalian, but I confess I have little love for bishops or presbyteries. I cannot fathom God's purpose and believe that no one else can, even the mighty divines of the Church. I was more antagonistic towards them in my years of grief. It was not God who helped me but my young daughter and friends who made my life worth living.'

Scougall was silent. He could not comprehend this viewpoint.

'Alas, I see the question of religion troubles you Davie. I think, therefore, it is a subject we should avoid for the moment. Let your mind wander from such things and return to this world. Have you had any further thoughts upon the matter in hand?'

Scougall was relieved to think about something else.

'The accounts given by Sir Lachlan's two men,' said Scougall, 'do they agree?'

'Yes – they remember seeing the chief return to his chamber. They drank the rest of the wine and both slept soundly in the small room next to Sir Lachlan's. I have spoken to them and they recall nothing remarkable about the evening. Nor, unsurprisingly, given the amount of drink they had consumed, did they hear anything until the morning.'

'Is it possible that they were involved in the killing?'

'Possible, but they had both served Sir Lachlan for more than twenty years. Duncan MacKenzie was his father's servant and Gregor McIan a landless man who had followed him since the days of the Covenant. Their wives, children and grandchildren have quarters in Glenshieldaig Castle. The future of their families depended on Sir Lachlan. It is not clear what they could gain from such an act. Sir Lachlan was liked by his servants. He paid well and stood by them. Hector is unlikely to be so generous.'

'This whole process is leading nowhere,' said Scougall peevishly. He was beginning to feel tired and sore after their long journey on horseback.

MacKenzie recognised his friend's mood.

'Davie, it has been a long day for you. We will soon be in Perth, where we can rest.'

CHAPTER 23
Dunkeld Cathedral

ANN MACLEAN EMERGED from the inn beside the mercat cross of Dunkeld wearing a black cloak over a blue dress, her hair not tied up but left to fall on her shoulders.

She wandered up a lane leading off the main street of the small burgh to a high set of iron gates, which she opened to enter the grounds of a large kirk. The cathedral was a huge structure for such a remote area of the country. The main part of the building was in a dilapidated state and most of the roof had collapsed. Ann thought how much the Reformers had to answer for – the destruction of beauty, all carried out by men. That vile Knox, the way he had treated his queen. She had attended mass in secret in London and their king was now an open Catholic – might she not find more peace in the old faith of Scotland? However, there was also an emotive grandeur in the ruinous state of the old kirk. Her eyes moved to the huge pine trees growing on the grassy bank and then to the mighty river.

She made her way through the trees, stopping now and then to touch the bark of the vast creations, or to stand with her back to one, and stare directly upwards until she felt dizzy, watching the highest branches sway in the breeze. She reached the bank and looked on the Tay. The river was wide, deep and in spate, for it had been raining in the mountains to the north and west. Its power had a magical attraction for her. She stood bewitched by the dark waters tumbling past, reflecting on the fleeting mystery of life; she considered her father's death and how the end of one life might, paradoxically, enhance and enrich another. She recalled the last words he had spoken to her: 'Your mother will be pleased with the result – a picture of a real Highland laird to remember me when I am dead.' His words had been prophetic, for the portrait painted of him by Henryson in Highland dress had turned out to be the last image of him. She felt a mixture of grief and annoyance which gave way to guilt. There were tears in her eyes.

No wonder the men of old had built their church in such a place beside these vast trees and this great river. She wanted to watch the water forever; the countless eddies on the river's surface, the turns and fluxes signifying to her the strange movements of fate.

A salmon broke from the water not far from where she stood. For an instant she saw the long silver body of the fish before it fell back into the black river. The splash ended her reverie and she remembered why she was there. Smiling at her absentmindedness, she quickly retraced her steps through the pines to enter a side door of the ruined kirk.

Light poured through the ribs of the roof, but some corners remained in darkness. She entered an area of shadow and found herself beside a tomb with a stone effigy of a knight lying on top of it. She could just make out the inscription in the gloom. It told her that the man buried there was the Wolf of Badenoch, an infamous member of the royal family, who had brought havoc to the Highlands hundreds of years before. She let her finger move from his spurs along his armoured leg and up to a stone thigh. What had this knight been like as a man?

Suddenly she was grabbed by a figure who emerged from the shadows. A hand smothered her mouth. She could not scream. Panic seized her and she struggled, but as her head fearfully turned to look at her assailant she met eyes she recognised, and, feeling his strong body against her, sought his lips. For a few moments they kissed and then emerged into the light beside the altar.

George Scott spoke softly: 'Are you sure no one saw you?'

'I'm sure. All the men are resting after our journey from Perth. Most of the town came out to welcome us. I had forgotten how beautiful this place is, Geordie.'

'Your brother would not be pleased by my presence here. Have you spoken to him yet?'

'I tried to do so as we rode here today, but he was cold and brooding, as he has been since Father's death. All he talks about are the finances of Glenshieldaig. He has said he must explore all possible avenues for raising money to save the House. I fear this means he wants to marry me to a local creditor, like my father did, or to the son of an English noblemen. Both prospects are vile to me, Geordie. I thought the destruction of my father would provide a more hopeful future for us – the prospect of a tocher if I married you. But my brother is becoming as stubborn as our father ever was! I do not know what we should do.'

'Come, let us take a short walk.'

Scott took her by the hand and led her out of the cathedral, looking around to make sure they were not being watched. They meandered through the trees. On the banks of the river he began to recite:

When Tayis bank was blumit bricht
With blossomes blyth and braid,
Be that river ran I doun richt,
Under the ryss I red.
The merle melit with all her micht,

And mirth in morning made,
Throw solace sound and seemly sicht,
Alswith a sang I said.

He fell silent and they both gazed at the river.

At last he spoke.

'We must not do anything hastily, Ann. Speak with your mother and brother when you reach Glenshieldaig. Convince them I do have reasonable prospects. I will get an income from the Army and some progress is being made in paying off the family's debts. At least we no longer have to deal with your father. He was a very difficult man. I cannot believe Hector will have such a cold heart.'

Ann kissed him again, long and passionately.

'Farewell, Geordie,' she breathed. 'Hopefully I will return to Edinburgh with good news. If not, we must make more desperate plans!'

CHAPTER 24
A Strange Meeting in Perth

WHEN THEY ARRIVED at the gates of Perth it was already growing dark. To Scougall's eyes the town appeared fairly unremarkable but as they made their way up the High Street he became aware that many of the inhabitants were speaking in Gaelic. The sound of this alien language filled him with foreboding. On reaching the Fair Maid, one of the burgh's more comfortable inns, they left their horses at the stable. MacKenzie greeted the innkeeper in Gaelic and introduced him to Scougall. The old man laughed as he heard the story of their journey and taking the young notary's hand, addressed him kindly, in English.

'You are most welcome here, Mr Scougall. Your rooms are ready but first you must take some food and drink. Before I forget, Mr MacKenzie, a letter was delivered for you this afternoon.'

MacKenzie took the letter and they sat themselves at a table by the small window.

'A note from Mr Stirling?' asked Scougall.

'No, Davie! From Campbell of Glenbeg! Read it for yourself.'

MacKenzie handed him the letter and Scougall read out:

'Dearest John, I will be in Black's Tavern tonight at eight. Your humble servant, Campbell of Glenbeg'.

'As usual, a man of few words,' remarked MacKenzie. 'Come, Davie, we have no time to dine. It is almost eight!'

'But, sir, how did he know where we were staying?'

'Glenbeg has many kinsmen in these parts. One of his clan probably spotted us on the road and informed him. *Cha nigh na tha dh'uisge sa mhuir ar càirdeas.* All the water in the sea won't wash out kinship! It is well known I usually spend the night here on my journeys north and south.'

'Surely you do not intend to meet with him? It is highly possible he is the murderer.'

'I doubt he will risk killing us both in Black's Tavern. We will visit our rooms quickly and I'll see you here in a few minutes. I will not wait – be hasty,' said MacKenzie.

The advocate seemed more animated than usual. Scougall wanted to go straight to bed and wished that he felt as excited about seeing Glenbeg again.

A few minutes later they were both outside the inn with MacKenzie leading the way along the High Street, down a gloomy vennel and into an even darker and grimier courtyard, where Black's Tavern was to be found. It was a filthy drinking den, lit only by a few, flickering candles.

'Black's is not one of Perth's most salubrious taverns,' MacKenzie commented unnecessarily. Scougall's expression held back none of his disgust. The fetid air was filled with a stench that seemed to burn his nostrils; he couldn't make out what the smell was, but reflected that the reek of simple beasts was far preferable to the odour of debauched men.

At one end of the small, low-ceilinged room sat Campbell of Glenbeg. His morose face, long white wig and tattered clothes depressed Scougall further. They had to pick their way over the body of a drunkard lying in a pool of vomit at the entrance of the howf. Scougall almost tripped over the crumpled figure; the man groaned, rolled over and resumed his slumber.

'Archibald,' MacKenzie began, 'we have only just arrived in Perth.'

'I would have waited for you, John. Come take some wine. Two more glasses!' Glenbeg shouted to the innkeeper. 'You will surely have a glass tonight, Mr Scougall?'

Scougall was too fearful to say no and accepted the large glass when handed it. He noticed Glenbeg's spidery fingers, their skeletal quality, the back of his hands covered in small blue veins. He took a large draught of the red wine, not removing his eyes from the strange Highlander in case he was suddenly attacked with a hidden dirk. The wine tasted foul but it warmed his throat and, as it made its way down his gullet towards his stomach, he regained his composure.

'I will come straight to the point,' Glenbeg commenced. 'I must declare first that I had no part in Sir Lachlan's murder. He was one of my few friends – he understood me like no other, we were creatures afflicted by the same passions. Drink and the table were shared vices, although I have pursued my pleasures with more zeal. At times I have sunk beyond madness to a place where nothing matters – where there is no difference between good and evil. But I talk too much of metaphysics, gentlemen. I played no part in Sir Lachlan's killing. I owed him some money, that's true, but I owe another hundred men money, and am I to kill a hundred men? I have evaded the arms of melancholia these last two years, though I am prepared to admit that when I lay trapped in that black crevice, murder seemed like a game and, God forgive me, I have killed... but I say again, I did not slay Sir Lachlan.'

Scougall was appalled that the man had freely admitted to breaking one of the Lord's Ten Commandments – Thou shalt not kill. The image of Moses calmed the young notary.

'Then why did you flee from Edinburgh?' he blurted out. The wine was beginning to give him some courage.

'My mind played tricks on me. I was certain I would be blamed. And so I left Edinburgh that morning. I have been here ever since.'

'Are you aware a warrant has been issued for your arrest?' asked MacKenzie.

'I have escaped the sheriff and his fools many times before.'

'You do not fear being seen in here?' asked Scougall.

'My clansmen will look after me, Mr Scougall.'

'I need to find out what you can remember about the night of Sir Lachlan's death. Did you see or hear anything that might shed some light on this affair?' MacKenzie enquired.

'I think not. It seemed like any one of the thousand nights I have spent at the table. Only one thing retains a place in my memory. As I left Hector MacLean told me that when his father died the House of Glenshieldaig would no longer support Campbell of Glenbeg. When he was chief there would be no more loans. His father had always helped me. He was a true friend, never taking me to court when I was unable to meet interest or principal. I now fear that Hector will begin proceedings against me as soon as he can, for he is strong for getting value for money and improving the finances of the estates.'

'This was all that Hector said to you?' asked MacKenzie.

Glenbeg nodded.

'Were you the last to depart?'

'I was. I had some business to discuss with Sir Lachlan. I hoped he might stand surety for me in a bond I intended to give to an Edinburgh merchant. Even Smith had retired to his chamber. After I left I walked up the High Street and turned into Hackerston's Wynd to take a nightcap at Maggie Rutherford's. I spent a couple of hours there and then retired to my lodgings in Craig's Wynd. A messenger arrived in the morning to tell me of Sir Lachlan's death and requesting I report to Mr Stirling at Smith's house. My memory of the previous night was dim. Stirling and I go back a long way. I saw that it would suit him and the Lord Advocate to place all the blame upon my head.'

'Have you any idea who might be responsible for killing our old friend?' asked MacKenzie.

'That I do not know. Like me, Sir Lachlan had many enemies. I have been fortunate to escape a number of attempts on my own life. Once, after a successful night at the table, a man I'd fleeced waited for me down a close and attempted to take me from behind, but I had sniffed him out and as he launched himself on me I raised the hilt of my sword to his face – he lost all his front teeth, top and bottom.' Glenbeg gave out a chilling laugh. 'Perhaps someone from Lachlan's past caught up with him, or a neighbouring chief decided to reignite a dormant feud. Now, gentlemen, I must leave. Be kind enough to tell that buffoon Stirling that he is chasing the wrong dog. I will travel to my clan lands, which I no longer possess but where I still have a few kinsmen who will protect their chief.'

The wine continued to work on Scougall.

'I have received intelligence that you dispatched a letter to Mr Smith which has cast the family into great distress,' he said boldly.

'I fear your intelligence is wanting. I have written no letters since I fled Edinburgh, except the small note I dispatched to you this evening,' the Highlander said with a menacing glare.

Glenbeg pulled himself up and readjusted his wig with his bony hands. Scougall caught sight of the baldness beneath. The Campbell offered his hand to them both and departed into the night.

'Some more wine, Davie?' MacKenzie filled his young friend's glass.

Scougall was on the verge of declining, but there was something about the taste that appealed to him. He liked the effect it was having: all kinds of questions were rushing into his mind.

'Do you believe Glenbeg, sir?' he began.

'I am not sure.'

'He admitted to other heinous crimes. Is it not conceivable that he lost himself in a drunken trance and killed Sir Lachlan?'

'I think that unlikely, Davie. Sir Lachlan's murder was carefully planned. Poison was administered. A search was made of his documents. The evidence suggests that Glenbeg played no part in Sir Lachlan's murder, but such men are never to be entirely trusted. They can never quench their thirst and may justify any deed to themselves.'

'Then he has provided us with little else to go on. We already knew that Sir Lachlan and Hector were on bad terms and he denied sending any letter to Smith.'

'Perhaps, Davie, perhaps.' MacKenzie was lost in thought for a few moments. 'Drink up, my boy, we have an early start in the morning and a long ride ahead of us.'

CHAPTER 25
Caterans

MACKENZIE AND SCOUGALL left Perth early the next morning and passed through Dunkeld, following the River Tay northwards. They were now truly in the Highlands. After a brief stop for a meal at the tiny settlement of Ballinluig on the River Tummel the weather turned; the blue sky disappeared, dark grey clouds rolled in from the north-west and it became much colder. When they entered the pass late in the afternoon Scougall was struck by the wildness of the scenery. The mist was soon descending.

'You are very quiet,' said MacKenzie.

'I was just thinking how lonely this glen is, sir.'

'Don't worry, we'll soon be through to Blair, where we can spend the night.'

They stopped beside a small burn, where MacKenzie dismounted and examined the embers of a fire and the carcass of a sheep. Mist now enveloped the glen in a cloak of white silence.

MacKenzie was sure he heard something. The wind picked up now and again to an eerie howl and as it died down there was a gentle pounding – a rhythmic sound. But tricks could be played on the hearing by the wind. No, again he could hear something, he was sure, but the mist obscured visibility beyond about half a mile.

'Davie, can you hear anything?'

Scougall dismounted and held his horse steady while he listened. He could make out nothing but the sigh of the wind.

But there it was again! The sound was coming from the direction of a copse of stunted trees about a hundred yards away on their left. A horseman suddenly appeared, followed by another, and another – six in total, heading towards them.

MacKenzie tried to remount, but was not as agile as he had been in his youth and by the time he had heaved himself into the saddle they were surrounded. Scougall's worst nightmares seemed to be taking flesh. Why had God forsaken him? The six Highlanders were a hellish sight with their matted hair and ragged plaids. The beardless one bore a huge scar on his neck. The thought passed through Scougall's mind that the man had survived the gallows.

'In God's name, who are they?' he whispered in terror.

MacKenzie said one word:

'Caterans!'

The harnesses of the lawyers' horses were quickly secured and the scarred man spoke to them in Gaelic. MacKenzie replied in his language, removed the pouch from his belt and indicated they might take the contents if they wished.

The conversation continued between MacKenzie and the scarred cateran. At last he translated the essence of what had been said for Scougall's benefit.

'They are broken men, Davie, men without a clan, who wander the glens seeking what they can find to live off – they will follow anyone who pays – and they have been paid to kill us.'

Scougall's heart froze. He closed his eyes and began to pray.

'They are willing to let us go if we can provide them with a larger sum. I have offered them all the cash in my possession, thirty pounds, but I don't think it is enough. Is there anything you have of value?'

Scougall shook his head.

MacKenzie then addressed the leader, again in Gaelic. Scougall was desperate to know what he was saying. The odd English word seemed to slip into their conversation: Court of Session... clerk... notary public, among a flood of impenetrable ones. MacKenzie was trying to convince them that the murder of a clerk of the Session would be a very serious offence and was not worth the sum of money they had been paid. But would they regard dispatching a lowly notary in the same light?

The scarred cateran gave orders to the others; his five comrades dismounted and slowly walked towards them. Scougall noticed their filthy legs – they wore plaids which left a significant part of their thighs exposed. He was pulled from his horse and he fell to the ground, expecting to feel the sharp thrust of a sword at any moment. One of the caterans grabbed him by the collar, pulled him up and, turning him round, raised a knife to his throat. Scougall felt the cold metal against his skin. His nostrils were infected by the foul smell of the Highlander's breath. His mind filled with a prayer that was more like a scream of despair.

MacKenzie was also being held at knife point, but the advocate was not calling on God, rather, he was trying to think of some argument he could employ to save their lives. A vision of his wife on their wedding day came to him, and with the image, bittersweet longing; the desire to touch her again, feel her flesh – was there an afterlife? Behind her were kinsfolk from both clans – Chisholms and MacKenzies – and in their midst his own chief, the Earl of Seaforth. He decided to play his only remaining card.

He raised his voice and began what was possibly the final

pleading of a long and distinguished career, telling them in Gaelic he was a great-grandson of MacKenzie of Kintail, the grandson of the Tutor of Kintail, and a noble of Clan MacKenzie. They would provoke the wrath of the entire kindred if they killed him and his young colleague.

MacKenzie's declaration appeared to have some effect. The caterans began to speak to each other and within a couple of minutes an argument had broken out which was only halted by the sound of horses approaching through the mist. Scougall continued with his prayers, for he thought that others were arriving to aid their murder.

About twenty horsemen emerged from behind a small knoll at the other side of the burn and crashed through the water. Mounted on fine horses, they were dressed in resplendent plaids. At the front was a big red-haired man who Scougall presumed was the leader of their assailants.

'MacGregors!' shouted MacKenzie.

Scougall took a sharp intake of breath. From the hands of caterans into the clutches of the most feared and despised Highland clan. God had certainly abandoned him now. His sins must have been grave! He wondered how he had transgressed.

The MacGregor chief spoke a few words of Gaelic and the knives were withdrawn from their necks. He turned to the scarred leader and the flow of Gaelic continued. Within seconds the six caterans were back on their horses. The chief moved from horse to horse collecting silver coins from each disgruntled man. Then he shouted a sharp command and they took off, vanishing into the mist.

He dismounted beside MacKenzie and taking him by the hand, greeted him warmly in Gaelic. Scougall was now on his knees, his whole body shaking at their close encounter with death.

'This is my assistant, Davie Scougall,' said MacKenzie, some calm restored to his voice. 'Davie, we have been most fortunate. Alistair MacGregor is a noble of the Clan MacGregor and an old friend. I have carried out much legal work for him over the years – often of a most delicate nature!'

Relief brought Scougall's hands to his head and he stumbled to the ground. It was astounding that MacKenzie was on friendly terms with a MacGregor chief and he was at a loss to know what to say to the man who had just saved his life.

'I can see you are both in a state of shock,' MacGregor said. 'I suggest you accompany us to our camp, where we can feed you and provide some comfort for the night.'

CHAPTER 26

A Late Drink in Ord's Tavern

HOPE, PRIMROSE AND Stirling sat at a table in a corner of the howf in Dunkeld; their black, tailored clothes contrasting with the grey, green and brown plaids of the other drinkers, who were mostly incomers to the small burgh – drovers, clansmen and other wanderers. Hope surveyed the scene and raised his large tankard to his companions:

'To a safe journey and a quick return to the Lowlands!'

The two lawyers held their glasses up to make the toast. Primrose was smartly dressed as usual, but he was suffering from a cold and was continually withdrawing a handkerchief from his pocket to blow his nose.

'I may be forced to resort to one of your remedies, Hope,' he spluttered.

'A sprig of rosemary, a few beads of sage and five small balls of horse dung added to some white wine and drunk at leisure. A most efficacious cure for all ailments of the throat. But I pray that it will have a more beneficial effect on you than it did on our old friend Sir Lachlan,' said the minister.

Archibald Stirling's face exuded worry from every pore. He was still thinking about the case and the reaction of the Lord Advocate if he had discovered nothing by the time of his return to Edinburgh. His wife's mood was also a concern. She did not understand why he had to make this sudden journey to the other side of the country. The only thought that brought him some cheer was that he was following in the footsteps of his hero. James Graham, the great Marquis of Montrose, had led a miraculous military campaign through the Highlands in 1644 and 1645.

'You appear ill at ease, Mr Stirling,' said Primrose. 'Take heart. I have heard that the Highlands are not as painful as many believe.'

Stirling smiled. 'The worries of a professional man, Mr Primrose. I have travelled through the Highlands many times and my impressions have generally been favourable. When I was your age, I was employed often by the Campbells of Glenmore, and made many visits to their residences.'

'I have heard the family has now fallen on hard times,' interjected Hope.

'That is correct – my client Sir Colin was little concerned with the management of his estates. All he desired was to secure a peerage from King Charles. He aspired to become a viscount or a marquis, believing that the family had reached such power and standing it deserved to be recognised. Sir Colin became so obsessed that everything was directed towards this end.'

'Vanity affects all such families. I believe that many years ago Sir Lachlan had hopes of a baronetcy,' said Hope.

The Crown Officer appeared to ignore him.

'Much of my work for Glenmore was taken up with the demands of this issue. When I think of the number of letters I had to write, each carefully making the case on behalf of Sir Colin and sent to scores of aristocrats and anyone who had interest at the Court in London. Despite all my efforts, he never secured anything. But I made money, as all good lawyers do. Sir Colin always told me each time I arrived in the Highlands – he rarely travelled to Edinburgh – that all he waited for in this life was a letter with good news from the King. I suppose much legal work, like so much human effort, is worthless.'

'Come now Mr Stirling,' said Hope, 'Let us not be cast down by melancholia on such a night. Like Mr Primrose, this is my first journey out of the Lowlands. Put such thoughts of woe from your mind and tell us something of your experiences so that we may be prepared for life at Glenshieldaig.'

'As I said, gentlemen, I was young. On my visits to Sir Colin all manner of sports were possible and I am sure the same will be the case at Glenshieldaig. Sir Colin's boat was given to us for fishing expeditions on Loch More. We also hunted in the mountains, but I am not skilled with either gun or bow and I had little success. The hunts were great gatherings: the chief, hundreds of clansmen and many of the neighbouring clans came together to kill and feast.' Stirling paused, then added, 'Sir Lachlan was a great man for hunting too, I believe.'

The three men fell silent and sat sipping their drinks until Primrose at last spoke: 'Mr Stirling, it pains me much to return to the subject, but have you learned anything significant about the killing of Sir Lachlan?'

'The affair appears as dark as ever,' said Stirling morosely, 'though my waking hours are spent on nothing else. The other night the ghastly faces of Sir Lachlan and Jossie appeared in my dreams. I have so little to go on. The disappearance of Glenbeg places suspicion on that scurrilous man, but I have no evidence of his involvement. It is no wonder my Lord Advocate grows weary. The Privy Council is now putting much pressure on his lordship, who then applies it to me. I have no appetite for such affairs at my age, gentlemen. Indeed, if I could afford to, I would retire as soon as this case is ended. I only hope that Mr MacKenzie has been luckier than I in his endeavours.'

'Why does MacKenzie meddle in such affairs? He is, after all, a potential suspect, as is his cohort, Mr Scougall,' said Hope. The minister's voice betrayed a degree of resentment that he would have preferred to hide.

'He is an honourable man and he acts with the authority of the kin of Sir Lachlan. I am glad of his work. He goes at it with a passion,' Stirling responded.

'In my opinion the most likely agent of the destruction of Sir Lachlan is Glenbeg,' Hope said. 'I have heard an interesting tale from a parishioner, who tells me that Glenbeg has been accused of murder before. On the Continent, after a commission had taken over his lands because of the miserable state of his finances, he became associated with an extreme group of sectaries known as the Children of Christ. They were convinced the apocalypse was imminent and that they had been chosen by God to proclaim the closeness of the event to the rest of mankind.'

The minister looked round the tavern to make sure they were not being listened to and lowered his voice.

'The details are sparse. Glenbeg was rescued by them following a grotesque period of debauchery. He was taken into their community destitute and provided with food and shelter. At some point thereafter he was converted to the cause, if only to secure some bread, and roamed the United Provinces preaching the end of the world. One night a member of the sect was accosted by a drunken soldier. Glenbeg was nearby. He withdrew the dirk he still carried with him and was on the soldier in an instant, stabbing the man in the stomach. He proceeded to tear the fellow's neck with his teeth. Glenbeg had to flee the local jurisdiction and leave his beloved brethren. Eventually he made contact with some clansmen who secured his return to Scotland. Since then he has begged his way round old acquaintances like Sir Lachlan, who were always too generous to the rascal.'

'I fear that such a tale cannot be used as evidence in our courts,' said Stirling.

'I have heard a similar story, Mr Stirling,' Primrose interjected, 'and I'm sure there must be something in this. A man who can rip out another's throat could murder again.'

'Perhaps you are right,' replied the Crown Officer.

'Now, gentlemen, it grows late and we must rise early tomorrow for we depart at sunrise. I suggest we take to our beds,' said Primrose, yawning.

CHAPTER 27
MacGregors

SCOUGALL SAT ON an animal fur beside a raging fire. This, presumably, was the 'bed' referred to by the MacGregor chieftain. Despite the warmth of the fire that crackled with considerable ferocity only a few feet away, he still felt chilled to the bone. The thought of the knife on his neck would not leave him. As he stared into the flames he thanked God for his deliverance, but cursed himself for agreeing to the journey in the first place. And now he was in the company of the most lawless clan of them all! And Alistair MacGregor was a client of MacKenzie! He looked at the Highlanders around the fire drinking and feasting on some kind of meat, apparently celebrating a good price for their cattle at the market in Falkirk.

The MacGregor chieftain and MacKenzie, who had been deep in conversation in Gaelic a little distance from the fire, came to join him.

'Now, gentlemen,' Alistair MacGregor began, 'it has been a close shave but you will soon feel better.'

'Thank you, Alistair. I have been travelling the drove roads to Ross-shire for over thirty years and this is the first occasion I've been attacked in this manner,' said MacKenzie, his usual sparkle of good humour missing.

'It will take time to recover – these men were sent to kill

you. It seems you have upset someone.'

'Are you familiar with the details of Sir Lachlan MacLean's death?' asked MacKenzie.

'News has reached us that he was poisoned, but the culprit remains unknown.'

'Mr Scougall and I have been on the trail of the killer – and we are now getting close for he, or she, has decided to destroy us as well. This is most disturbing, but at the same time it is an incentive. I am sure we are near to finding the identity of the murderer.'

'I have many spies in the Highlands, John, they will listen for intelligence. We had been trailing your attackers for a number of days. Such men are easy prey for us. If they have stolen a few cattle from a Lowland landowner, we will take them for ourselves. It is the way of things here, Mr Scougall. *Feumaidh na fithich fhèin a bhith beò*, as we say in Gaelic – the ravens themselves must live.'

'Who were the caterans?' Scougall at last broke his silence.

'Ah! I see your assistant does speak!' said MacGregor, a half smile on his lips. 'Their life is one of wandering from glen to glen, seeking what they can,' he continued. 'Sometimes they venture into the Lowlands where they make cattle raids or take whatever else they can lay hands on. They were tenants once, or followers of a particular chief, but have lost all claim to tenancy or have been banished from their clan. The government in Edinburgh believes we MacGregors are broken men, but we still survive as a kin despite being harried by the Clan Campbell these last two hundred years. Some of us have even been forced to change our names and till the lands of the hated Campbells. Others, like ourselves, roam these lonely glens and make of life what we can.'

He broke off and looked closely at the young notary, as if

to discern what impression his words were making.

'Mr Scougall, it is too easy to judge these caterans by your Lowland standards. Life in the Highlands is difficult. As you see, the land produces little. Rain and wind are our constant companions. And some of us have been slow in changing. We have not followed clans like the MacKenzies and the Campbells into the Lowlands to the very heart of government and the law. We cling to the old ways.'

MacGregor turned to address MacKenzie.

'John, many of your clansmen are now rich lawyers in Edinburgh – a number are notaries; a few, like yourself, are advocates; some like Rosehaugh have achieved even higher positions. This has given your clan many advantages. But we MacGregors have not followed this path, partly because of persecution, and also because we have our pride. We care not for Lowland ways. We wish our children to speak Gaelic and to be educated at our own schools – not in the Lowland burghs. But the story of the MacGregors is indeed a long and sorry one, and I fear Mr Scougall is perhaps not in the mood for Highland history.'

The MacGregor chieftain indicated that he wanted a word with MacKenzie in private. The two men moved away from the fire and their conversation continued in Gaelic. Scougall did not understand the words that he could barely hear.

It was now pitch dark and most of the clansmen were at the fire. Scougall looked around nervously and was relieved to see a number of men posted to keep watch.

'Don't be concerned, Mr Scougall,' said MacGregor, who had returned to sit beside him. 'My men have keen ears and caterans would not dare risk making an attack on us, even for two thousand pounds!'

Bowls of brose were passed to them. Scougall forced himself to eat despite his lack of appetite.

MacKenzie was right, he thought, this attempt on their lives showed the killer was scared.

'It is the custom that our bard should provide entertainment after a meal. Are you a Gaelic speaker, Mr Scougall?'

'I speak not one word, sir.'

'Then I will translate for you. Sit close beside me and as he recounts the story I will whisper the words in English into your ear.'

CHAPTER 28
Arrival at Glenshieldaig

FORTUNATELY THE JOURNEY thereafter was uneventful. The following day they reached Blair Castle, where they spent a comfortable night, although MacKenzie's client, the Marquis of Atholl, was not in residence. The next morning they left before dawn and made good progress. They caught up with the chief's cortège in the late afternoon. In the evening they set up camp by a deep loch below precipitous mountains, and there they were joined by Hope, Primrose and Stirling with two Highland guides who had taken another droving route from the south.

The expanded party continued through the high mountains of the West Highlands. Scougall was still tense and taciturn, even with his fellow Lowlanders. But as the impact of the incident with the caterans began to fade in intensity, he became more aware of the bleak beauty of his wild surroundings.

At last they reached the top of the pass. Before them lay waves of hills descending to the sea, and, towards the horizon, the silhouettes of islands with their own high peaks. Scougall gazed in amazement – he had seen nothing like it before. In the far distance he could just make out a black castle on what looked like a small island near the shore.

'What is that?' he asked MacKenzie, pointing to it.

'That is the end of our journey, Davie – Glenshieldaig

Castle. You are very fortunate, for most do not see it for the first time in such fine weather. It is indeed a magnificent vista from this vantage point.'

'How old is the castle, sir?'

'Hector, I am sure, can give you a full history.'

The young chief was standing beside the two lawyers, staring mournfully towards the sea. He spoke curtly, without looking at Scougall.

'It was built by the Lord of the Isles and came into the hands of MacLean of Duart at a later date, and then to our family. My father made many alterations to the structure and spent a pretty penny on making it comfortable. Henryson travelled all the way from Edinburgh to paint the ceilings, which are regarded as the finest in the West Highlands. My father bought exquisite hangings from the Continent and furniture from England, France and Holland. Unfortunately the lands are mortgaged to the hilt.'

Hector abruptly mounted his horse and trotted to the front of the cortege to join his sister and clansmen. MacKenzie and Scougall remained at the rear in the company of Primrose, Stirling and Hope as they slowly proceeded down the track towards the sea. None of the Highlanders spoke as a mark of respect for their dead chief's return to his ancestral home.

It took them two hours to reach the machair. Scougall noticed that this area of flat grassland beside the sea was home to what seemed like hundreds of wild flowers. The air was full of birdsong. The local people assembled to witness the return of the chief stood at the side of the muddy track, heads bowed in silence as the party passed with the body of Sir Lachlan, then joined the procession that slowly wound its way along the shore towards Glenshieldaig Castle. Scougall's attention was taken by the aspect of these folk; dressed in dark plaids, they paid their respects in what he regarded as a most dignified way, only a few children breaking the silence.

They passed through a small township. Scougall was fascinated by the simple dwelling places: stone walls perhaps only five feet high, low wooden doors and two tiny windows beneath peat roofs.

At last the castle came into clearer view. It was built on a rocky islet perhaps a hundred yards from the shore. Reached by a narrow causeway, it was in essence a stone keep – a defensive block of stone with no windows, only the odd arrow slit in irregular positions. Its architecture forcibly impressed on Scougall that violence was still at the heart of life here. For him, the castle's stark walls of black stone recalled the cold metal of the cateran's dirk.

When Hector MacLean and his kinsmen reached the causeway they halted their horses and waited silently for a few minutes. The gate of the castle was opened and a woman dressed in black appeared. She walked slowly towards the coffin. At a distance, the gracefulness of her bearing caused Scougall to imagine she was young. As she came closer, however, he realised she was older but nevertheless beautiful, with long dark hair falling to her shoulders. She embraced her son and daughter and greeted her husband's kinsmen; then, bowing her head in the direction of the coffin, she turned and retraced her steps back towards the castle. The procession followed her, the sound of hooves echoing on the stone.

When she reached the castle the gates were opened fully and the cart bearing Sir Lachlan's body, followed by thirty horsemen, entered the courtyard.

The rest of the clan remained on the other side. Scougall walked across behind MacKenzie, his eyes cast down, observing the rock pools and black seaweed in the shallows. He was reminded of carefree days on the beach near his home. How far he had travelled in the space of a few weeks.

CHAPTER 29

The Great Hall of Glenshieldaig

THE HUGE TAPESTRIES depicting Biblical scenes hanging from the walls of the Great Hall of Glenshieldaig Castle took Scougall's thoughts back to the night when Sir Lachlan had been killed, when they had all sat around Smith's oak table, playing cards. The ceiling in Sir Lachlan's Edinburgh lodgings was decorated in a similar manner. Scougall felt guilty. He had been the only one not to drink more than a glass of wine and should have been able to give MacKenzie at least one detail which would help to provide an answer to this dark puzzle. If only he could remember more clearly the events of that evening. He shut his eyes and took himself back to his arrival at the tenement. He remembered following MacKenzie up the stairs to the third floor; knocking on the door; Sir Lachlan welcoming them both warmly; walking through to the chamber; sitting beside Primrose; listening as Sir Lachlan praised his lawyers for their success in the Session.

A nudge from MacKenzie startled him and he opened his eyes. For an instant he forgot where he was, as if awoken from a deep sleep, and spoke out loudly: 'The answer lies at the table in Smith's house!'

MacKenzie held the elbow of his young friend until Scougall regained his composure, the redness of his cheeks betraying his embarrassment. MacKenzie indicated they were to walk forward and Scougall followed him. They had been waiting in a line to greet Sir Lachlan's widow, who stood beside the coffin in the chapel off the Great Hall – a small windowless room with a vaulted ceiling, whitewashed walls and a few silver candles. Scougall was relieved by the simple appearance – no suggestion of popery! Sir Lachlan's coffin seemed to take up the greater part of the room, just like the chief himself. Larger than life, even in death.

MacKenzie embraced Tibbie MacLean and beckoned Scougall forward. The young notary was ill at ease, unsure what to say to the chief's wife. But before he could ponder too long, MacKenzie had introduced him and he found himself being embraced by a tall woman who was older than his mother, but whose startling brown eyes had an alluring power.

'Mr Scougall, thank you for travelling so far to pay your respects to my husband. I hope your journey was not too uncomfortable and you will return from Glenshieldaig with a favourable disposition towards life here.'

She spoke slowly, in a soft melodic voice, as if reminding herself how to speak in English.

Scougall was still lost for words. MacKenzie came to his rescue.

'Tibbie, I am deeply sorry – he will be missed by many.' MacKenzie paused. 'I regret I must talk of business at such a time but I am sure that Hector has told you there is much to be done so that the affairs of the estate can be put in order. Mr Scougall and I are here as your servants and we would be very grateful if you could allow us to examine Sir Lachlan's papers. As you know, a number of creditors cry out for money on the expectation that Hector will be a better payer than his father.'

Tibbie MacLean gave MacKenzie her hand, which he took and held between his own. 'It is very good to see you again, John – it has been too long since you last visited Glenshieldaig.

Mr Primrose will give you the key of the charter kist.'

They were directed forward by one of the servants. A painting of the dead chief had been placed on the coffin. The likeness was very good. Sir Lachlan stood in Highland dress with red and black chequered hose, a plaid of brown and red tartans hung over one arm. He wore a richly embroidered short jacket and a large black hat from which a single white feather drooped. A small dirk with jewelled handle was hanging from his belt and in his right hand was a long musket which rested on the ground. Scougall realised the chief had been painted in John Smith's house, but the artist had transferred the setting to Sir Lachlan's own bedchamber in Glenshieldaig Castle. At one side of the chief was a small table on which rested a book, a linen kerchief and a wine glass. On the other, behind the musket, was a window which opened onto a view of Highland hills; a few stags were just visible in the distance.

'This is the painting Henryson completed on the afternoon of the murder,' said MacKenzie, who moved forward to get a closer look, his eyes coming to rest on the table. He could just make out the words written on the leather cover of the book, 'The Conquests of King Alexander', while on the kerchief was a tiny embroidered insignia which appeared to be a galley, and on the side of the glass were the initials 'LM'.

MacKenzie and Scougall were directed out of the chapel by a servant and found themselves back in the Great Hall with Hope and Primrose. The key of Sir Lachlan's charter chest was provided by the young advocate who smiled as he passed it to MacKenzie.

'I believe there will be much work required to establish order in the morass of Sir Lachlan's papers – I bid you good luck, gentlemen,' he said.

'Come, Davie, we obviously have much to do. Let us make haste,' said MacKenzie.

They walked down a long passage, up a narrow spiral stairway for two flights, and into a room which, when they lit their candles, revealed account books, ledgers and legal papers from floor to ceiling and a large kist at the far side. Placing the iron key in the lock, MacKenzie turned it with considerable difficulty and heaved open the top of the chest.

'Now, Davie, the keen eyes of a young notary are required!'

'But what are we looking for, sir?'

'Ah! We will not know until we have found it! I suggest you take off your cloak and prepare for a long afternoon. *Buinnigear buaidh le foighidinn* – patience wins victory.'

MacKenzie divided the documents he removed from the chest into two groups.

'There, Davie – one for you and one for me.'

There was only one small table and a solitary chair in the room. MacKenzie lifted up a bundle and placed them on the table. Scougall was forced to sit on the floor with his pile. He took the document from the top and began to read.

It was a long afternoon. Time passed at a snail's pace. The two lawyers did not talk as they sat over the documents. Scougall's thoughts drifted now and again to the grim face of Glenbeg or the cateran's blade. MacKenzie was thinking about Tibbie MacLean thirty years before – she had been such a beauty – she still was.

The sun was low in the sky when Scougall sighed deeply and said, 'I have found nothing out of the ordinary in any of these documents, sir. Every charter, instrument and bond appears as it should. I fear we are wasting our time here.'

'Perhaps you are right. Even so, I still believe the documents that were disturbed in Sir Lachlan's chamber in Edinburgh have some bearing on this case.'

CHAPTER 30
Refreshments in the Great Hall

TWO HOURS LATER they decided to abandon work for the night and made their way back to the Great Hall where kinsmen and guests seated at long wooden tables were enjoying an evening meal. The smell of roasted meats including beef, chicken, rabbit and venison was enticing. The room was aglow as the dark red tapestries seemed to exude the warmth of the raging fire. By the great stone fireplace sat Sir Lachlan's family and the Lowland guests.

'Welcome,' said Tibbie MacLean. 'Please be seated. I can see from your bleary eyes you've spent an hour too many on my husband's documents. Forget legal business for a while and join us.'

MacKenzie and Scougall returned the greeting and took their seats.

'I have already made a brief survey of Sir Lachlan's papers and all appears in order,' said Primrose before biting vigorously into a chicken leg.

'Yes,' replied MacKenzie, 'Hector will succeed to the lands and dignities of Glenshieldaig without much delay.'

'I'm afraid there is little dignity still attached to the House of Glenshieldaig! My father has left his estate in such an afflicted state. Unless I take action to remedy the situation, I will be unable to travel to Edinburgh again without fear of arrest,' said Hector MacLean in a cold voice.

There was silence around the table for a few moments following the young chief's outburst.

'Have you found out anything further about my father's murder?' Ann MacLean directed her question to Mr Stirling rather than MacKenzie.

'Our enquiries are continuing, my lady. Glenbeg has been spotted in Perth – it is only a matter of time before he is apprehended and questioned. He has few friends left in the Highlands.'

'Please, Mr Stirling,' interrupted Tibbie MacLean, her voice revealing her grief, 'let us not talk of such things until my husband is laid to rest, especially not now, on the night before his funeral. I wish only to think of him as he was, and not dwell further on the terrible events in Edinburgh.'

'I am sorry.' Ann placed her hand on her mother's and clasped it tightly.

The chief's widow beckoned one of the servants to bring a large earthenware bottle to the table and filled everyone's drinking vessels.

'Gentlemen, join us in toasting my husband's life.'

They all raised their quaichs and drank to the memory of the chief. Thirsty after his long session in the charter room, Scougall finished the contents in one go, only to lurch forward in a fit of coughing – his chest was on fire!

'Davie! Another new experience for you – real Highland whisky!'

'I thought it was wine. It is burning my very insides!'

Scougall took deep breaths until the urge to vomit diminished. He felt he was revealing himself as an imbecile at every turn.

'I am deeply sorry my lady,' he said, addressing Tibbie MacLean, 'for degrading the memory of your husband.'

'Do not worry, Mr Scougall – my husband would approve. He was always pleased to see a lawyer in difficulties,' she said with a wry smile. 'Now, gentlemen, an announcement! Mr Primrose has just informed us that he is to be married to the younger daughter of the Earl of Boortree.'

Primrose looked even more smug than usual.

'A most beautiful and gentle creature. I am convinced she will make me a better man,' he said with false modesty.

'And her father's influence will not hold back your legal career,' said Hope.

'She is a perfect match,' Primrose simpered.

'If only my children could be as fortunate – the issue of marriage has brought nothing but trouble to this house,' Tibbie MacLean sighed.

Ann looked coldly at her brother, then away.

'Do you have any plans to marry, Mr Scougall?' Tibbie asked.

The image of MacKenzie's daughter came into his mind.

'I have begun to give it serious attention, yes.' After downing the whisky he was in danger of becoming loquacious. 'I am now four and twenty years old. I have devoted my entire life to the law…'

'And golf,' interjected MacKenzie. 'He plays a better wood than any lawyer I know in Edinburgh.'

'I must now consider marriage more seriously, for I can think of no more perfect union than that between man and woman under God…' His habitual self-consciousness suddenly returned.

'I had expected Mr Smith might also have travelled to Glenshieldaig,' MacKenzie said, turning to Hope.

'It appears he has received some bad news. His sister-in-law in Perth has died unexpectedly. Smith's wife has taken it badly. They were very close. The burgess is unable to leave her at the moment.'

Scougall remembered their conversation with Glenbeg. Perhaps the lank Highlander was telling the truth and Peggy had misheard her master's words. He looked at MacKenzie, who appeared to be deep in thought.

After the meal was finished and a number of further toasts drunk to Sir Lachlan, the MacLeans of Glenshieldaig and the MacLeans of Duart, Tibbie accompanied them to the door. Scougall was by now swaying slightly. A painting on the wall facing appeared to loom up towards him – another portrait of Sir Lachlan, but in early middle age. For the first time he realised that the chief had been a handsome, powerful man. There was no sign of the large bags under his eyes and his hair was dark brown rather than grey.

'John, I think it may be of importance to mention to you that my husband kept another small box of documents in his private chamber. I am not sure of his reasons for doing so. Here are the keys. The casket can be found in the cabinet beside the bed,' said the chief's widow. She spoke in a low tone, her tired eyes and drawn face betraying the devastation of her loss.

'Has anyone else had access to these keys, Tibbie?' asked MacKenzie, staring intently at her.

'No one. I only remembered its existence a few moments ago when…'

'Tibbie, I would be pleased if you would not mention this casket to anyone else until I have had time to look through its contents.'

'Of course.'

'Do your children know anything of it?'

'I am sure they do not, for my husband was careful in hiding it in his private chamber. I don't think he ever talked about it with my son.'

Tibbie returned to her place at the table beside her son and daughter, who were deep in conversation.

'Davie, our work is not yet over for the day,' MacKenzie said urgently. 'We must be quick before tiredness robs us of our faculties. Unfortunately you have partaken too liberally of the *uisge-beatha* – not an ideal preparation for the study of legal documents!'

'I am perfectly well sir,' slurred Scougall, 'I am in complete command of my faculties.' He almost tripped as he followed the advocate out of the Great Hall.

CHAPTER 31
The Contents of the Casket

SIR LACHLAN'S CHAMBER was an opulently furnished room at the top of the castle. The walls were covered with arras hangings of dark red, depicting hunting scenes. An ornately carved four-poster bed with a magnificent crewel-work bedspread was the central feature; the rest of the furniture comprised a number of chairs and a couple of small tables. A wooden cabinet in the Dutch style stood beside the bed. MacKenzie tried one of the tiny keys, but it did not fit and he used the second one. The door of the cabinet opened. Inside was a small casket, perhaps a foot in length, half as broad, and finely carved from the same wood as the bed.

Scougall stared down at the exotic carving on the lid of the casket. It seemed to represent a series of human bodies. He was shocked to discover that he was looking at a carnal entangling of a number of men and women. He was about to draw MacKenzie's attention to the libidinous nature of the work of art, which was surely the creation of some depraved craftsman from the Orient, when the advocate slipped the small key into the lock and opened it to reveal a roll of parchment tied with a thin piece of leather. MacKenzie carefully loosened the thong and the coiled paper fell apart to reveal a number of separate documents.

Scougall's attention wandered to a gruesome depiction of a

wolf hunt on one of the hangings. He recalled with a frisson of fear that such beasts still roamed the hills around the castle.

MacKenzie laid six documents on the table at the foot of the bed. He looked down on the ochre parchments, focusing hard on each word.

'Instruments of sasine relating to tracts of land purchased by Sir Lachlan,' said Scougall, peering over his shoulder.

'Very good, Davie.'

'They appear to be adequate examples of the notary's art. I can see nothing particular in them. Who was the writer?'

'Gavin Hamilton, the clan notary of the MacLeans of Glenshieldaig who served Sir Lachlan for a generation. He died only a few years ago.'

Scougall glanced down again at one of the documents, checking that all the clauses were in order and then examining the witness list. Forgetting himself, he began to read the names of the witnesses: 'Sir Lachlan MacLean of Glenshieldaig, John MacLean of Kinlochard, Sir Roderick MacKenzie of Ardcoul, Kenneth MacKenzie of Gairlochhead, Gavin Hamilton, notary public, dated the 12th day of October 1642 at Glenshieldaig.'

MacKenzie turned to him, his voice betraying his excitement.

'Read the witness list again,'

Scougall did so, emphasising each word and trying not to slur.

'That's it!' MacKenzie exclaimed.

'What, sir?' Scougall could discern nothing unusual in the list.

'Sir Roderick MacKenzie of Ardcoul is my father – he died in 1639. This document is dated 1642! The instruments are forgeries! Well done, Davie Scougall! The whisky encouraged you to read aloud and it has jarred my mind into activity at this late hour. We must take them down to the charter room so we can compare the signatures.'

The room where they had spent the afternoon was now icily cold. The fire had burnt out. It was approaching midnight. The advocate's fingers searched through the contents of the chest until he found the document he was looking for.

'Davie, this instrument is dated 1638. Look at the witness list.'

Scougall read from the document: 'Sir Lachlan MacLean of Glenshieldaig, John MacLean of Kinlochard, Sir Roderick MacKenzie of Ardcoul, Kenneth MacKenzie of Gairlochhead, Gavin Hamilton, notary public.'

'Now, examine the signatures.'

MacKenzie placed the document from the casket beside the instrument from which he had just read. At first glance the signatures looked identical, but as Scougall's eyes moved from one to the other he discerned subtle differences. The forger had made a good job.

'What does all this mean, sir?' he asked.

'I am not quite certain yet. I must keep these papers with me tonight. I fear the forger might wish them destroyed. We will have to leave something else in their place. Have you any papers on you?'

'Only some theological reflections I have copied from Grundy.'

'Ah, your favourite author! Well, that will have to do.'

Scougall removed a wad of crumpled paper from his leather pouch and handed it to MacKenzie, who rolled it up carefully, tied it with the leather thong and placed it in the casket, which he returned to the cabinet.

'Come, we must get some sleep. It has been a very long day and I suspect that tomorrow will be a testing one.'

When Scougall returned to his chamber he checked that the door was firmly bolted, then opened the small window and stuck out his head. Cool night air and the smell of the sea reminded him of his home in Musselburgh. It was a moonless night and he could not see the ocean, but he could hear the gentle lapping of the waves against the castle rock some fifty feet below.

After a few minutes he closed the window, lay on his bed and tried to make sense of the events of the day. Before he came to any conclusions, he had fallen asleep.

CHAPTER 32
A Late Guest Arrives

SCOUGALL WOKE SUDDENLY. The pain in his head was acute, his mouth as dry as he could remember. He must get some water!

He staggered to his feet and in the darkness tried to find the jug on the table at the other side of the room. His hand knocked into something which crashed to the ground and he felt coldness on his legs. He groaned – the water was spilt. It was the middle of the night and he could not call a servant in such a condition. He would have to make his way down to the kitchens to get some more.

He groped towards the door, found the bolt and was out into the corridor. At least a candle was burning on a metal bracket on the wall. His journey would not be in complete darkness.

He walked along a half-lit passageway until he reached the top of a stairwell and began to descend, fearful that he might slip on the damp stones that spiralled downwards.

He heard a sound. Unsure if it came from within his own head, he stopped and listened. Yes – he was sure – someone was climbing upstairs towards him, one of the castle servants perhaps.

Scougall resumed his descent – round and round the tight spiral of stairs, down and down.

A figure suddenly came into view. The pale face encased in a white periwig was unmistakable. Scougall gasped. It was Archibald Campbell of Glenbeg!

Glenbeg's face in the ghostly half-light was terrifying. Scougall stood paralysed by fear.

'Mr Scougall, we meet again!' Glenbeg said coldly. He ascended until he was two steps below the young notary. The festering odour of alcohol wafted from the mouth of the wheezing Highlander into his face. Scougall thought he was going to vomit.

'Life is a strange game, Mr Scougall!'

Glenbeg's skeletal hand began to rise towards Scougall, who was transfixed by the hideous apparition. The Campbell was no longer wearing Lowland breeches and jacket but was clad in a dark green plaid tied with a leather belt around bony hips. From it, a Highland broadsword hung, the golden handle reflecting the candlelight. Scougall's mind flashed back to their previous meetings: the silent figure at Sir Lachlan's gaming table, the hunted man in the drinking den in Perth where he had confessed to committing murder. Scougall was now convinced that Glenbeg was Sir Lachlan's killer – there could be no doubt. But why was he roaming the gloomy passageways of Glenshieldaig castle during the night? Was he, Davie Scougall, notary public, to meet his end here in this dank stairwell? Were all his hours at the writing desk a preparation for this pathetic exit?

The gaunt Highlander's hand reached his ear. A forefinger moved down the side of his cheek. Scougall felt the long nail against the bristles on his face. Glenbeg smiled.

A finger was on his nape – then a hand slid round his neck. Glenbeg began to tighten his grip, the cheerless grin still in place, his eyes cold and deadly. The other hand rose and joined the act of strangulation. Scougall finally put his hands up to resist but the old Highlander was too strong for him. He felt his grip on consciousness start to ebb away.

Then he was aware of someone singing a Lowland air his mother had sung to him when he was a boy.

Sae gently I staw tae ma bonnie maid's chamber,
And rapped at her windae, low doon on ma knee;
Beggin that she would awauk frae sweet slumber,
Awauk frae sweet slumber an pity me.

The pressure on his neck was suddenly released and Glenbeg was past him and disappearing round the next bend in the staircase. Scougall's back slid down the outside wall and he ended up sitting on a stone slab. The large smiling face of Mr Hope loomed into sight.

The notary thanked God for the fat minister.

CHAPTER 33
A Nightcap

'JOHN, I'M SORRY to summon you at this late hour,' began Stirling, 'but I have important news. George Scott has been spotted in Dunkeld. A note he sent from there to Ann MacLean has been intercepted. If I may quote briefly from the first line of the letter: *My dearest Ann, now that your father is no longer here to thwart…*'

MacKenzie took a seat at the fire beside the Crown Officer. He was tired but knew it would take him a long time to sleep tonight: there was so much to think about and the discovery of the forgeries had exhilarated him. The pit was far off – out on the edge of his mind where he wanted it to be. Strenuous business kept those feelings at bay. The darkness would not come tonight, of that he was certain.

'I'm sure we have the killers, John. The contents of this note and the brooch you found at Jossie's shop are evidence enough. The motive is clear – Sir Lachlan stood in the way of their marriage. He would settle no tocher on his daughter if she wed George Scott. With the chief out of the way, a financial arrangement is possible with Hector. I have sent orders for Scott to be arrested and I intend to detain Ann MacLean after the funeral. Glenbeg it would seem is innocent.'

Stirling's feeling of grim resignation had gone; he was going to tie up the loose ends of the case and return home. He handed the note to MacKenzie, who read it quickly.

'Archibald, I fear the evidence is not conclusive,' he warned the Crown Officer. 'This letter from Scott is but a statement of fact and not a confession. Also, I have intelligence that the brooch I found can be bought in John Nisbet's shop for five shillings. It hardly seems the kind of piece to be worn by a lady who holds herself in such high esteem.'

'It seems clear enough to me, John!'

'Archibald, you must remain calm. I am sure we are very close to the end of the search. Give me one more day before you take any action. Keep your eyes on me at the funeral tomorrow. When I leave the graveside, follow me, but remain at a distance. If my suspicions prove correct, we will discover the identity of the killer.'

As MacKenzie rose to leave, he noticed a manuscript book on the table by the fire.

'I see you still work on your *History*. Did you know that I actually saw Montrose at Inverness in May 1650, after his capture – he was on a small horse with his feet fastened beneath wearing an old red plaid. The whole town turned out to see him. He was offered wine at the mercat cross but asked for water. I will never forget it – a great man.'

The subject of his hero animated Stirling.

'You must put your memories on paper so that I can use them, John. We all need heroes, especially during these troubled times – a leader to inspire us.' The Crown Officer thought of the lean figure of Rosehaugh. Such a man did not engender love or loyalty. 'Yes, John – ten years' effort so far.'

'When do you hope to publish?'

'Soon – when I find time for a little more revision. I must review certain parts of the narrative; revisit some of the main characters; delve deeper into the well of motivation.'

MacKenzie reflected that if his old friend could apply such

passion to the real world he would make a fine Crown Officer. But he knew only too well the alluring power of books – how a happier life could be led within the confines of literature. He understood the fascination of disentangling the mysterious web of history.

'I look forward to reading it very much, Archibald. It will be a great achievement. The one by which you will be remembered.'

CHAPTER 34
Sir Lachlan's Funeral

SCOUGALL STOOD IN the courtyard of the castle feeling wretched; his head was pounding and his body leaden with intense weariness. He cursed himself for drinking so much whisky. He should have known it could only result in humiliation. Why had he not stopped after the first toast? Was there not the example of his uncle? And now he had suffered the indignity of having to be roused by his master. After knocking on his door without answer, MacKenzie had pushed it open and found him slumped on his bed, fully clothed and barely able to move.

Losing control made Scougall hate himself. How was he to attend a funeral in such a state? His hair was uncombed, his jacket and breeches crushed and his eyes red. He rubbed his neck and thought of the cold hands of Glenbeg tightening like a vice. A cup of warm milk was all that he could stomach for breakfast. He begged God for forgiveness.

The courtyard was full of mourners preparing to follow the coffin to the family tomb. MacKenzie was speaking to Tibbie MacLean. He looked none the worse for their late night. Scougall had blurted out the tale of his horrific encounter with Glenbeg, the attempt on his life and the divine intervention of Mr Hope, but MacKenzie seemed to take these revelations with remarkable equanimity, merely asking him to hurry or they would be late.

The chief's widow was listening intently to MacKenzie and she looked worried. Hector MacLean stood solemnly some distance away. He was now the chief of Glenshieldaig, but the title had brought little wealth or happiness. Estate policy was everything to him.

Ann was standing behind her brother. Scougall noticed her resemblance both to Sir Lachlan and his wife; she was beautiful but also haughty and he found this unattractive. It was difficult to believe she was capable of two murders, but she and Scott would not be the first lovers in history to be driven to commit such acts.

His gaze shifted to the other side of the courtyard, where the two Edinburgh lawyers, Primrose and Stirling, were deep in conversation. Primrose was not a likeable man, thought Scougall, despite his fine coats, good looks, eloquence and prospective marriage to the Earl of Boortree's daughter. There was something calculating in his demeanour – such a man was surely capable of anything – but he had no apparent motive and he was known as a scrupulous lawyer. Primrose turned to address Mr Hope, who had just arrived. Scougall reflected that before meeting MacKenzie he would not have believed a man of the church could be implicated in such a crime, but the interview with Hope after Sir Lachlan's death, in which he had confessed so readily to fornication and duplicity, had raised doubts in his mind, although the minister's intervention last night had altered his opinion somewhat. Hope had practically carried him back to his chamber and deposited him on his bed.

Or was it Glenbeg? Scougall was suddenly struck with doubt. Had he only dreamt about their meeting on the stairwell?

He observed Sir Lachlan's two men beside the wooden cart on which the chief's coffin rested. They had been drunk on the night of the murder. They were ugly, shiftless looking creatures, uncivilised and godless, speaking only the barbaric Gaelic tongue. Scougall's eyes wandered round the others in the courtyard: kinsmen of Sir Lachlan, neighbouring chiefs, lairds and tenants. The faces of all took on a greyish hue under the overcast sky. He began to feel worse and shut his eyes. His forehead was glistening with cold sweat. It was important to clear his mind. He must think of the goodness in people. Despite the attack by the caterans, he had met with goodwill and genuine hospitality on his journey through the Highlands and at Glenshieldig Castle. MacKenzie was right. He must dispel the prejudices of his upbringing and adhere to arguments based on reason. But then the cadaverous features of Campbell of Glenbeg came into his mind again – the skeletal hands at his throat – the reek of his breath.

Scougall opened his eyes – a chink of blue was visible in the sky and he felt momentarily cheered. Everyone began to line up behind the cart on which the coffin rested. At the front of the procession were Tibbie with her son and daughter, then kinsmen of Sir Lachlan, followed by other chiefs – at the back were friends and Lowland guests. MacKenzie appeared at his side.

'Come this way, Davie. We will walk with Mr Primrose and Mr Stirling.'

The cart was pulled slowly out of the courtyard by a pair of black horses. The mourners followed through the wooden gates and across the causeway. A large crowd was waiting at the other side: the people of the clan, vassals and tenants of every rank, who had come to say a final farewell to the father of their family. Scougall was again surprised by the size of the throng, there were over a couple of thousand present to pay their last respects. As the cart passed through them, he heard women weeping and wails of despair. The procession proceeded up a dirt track for a mile or so then descended a small incline to the burial ground, where views opened up inland towards the peaks of the great mountains of the western Highlands and out to the islands of the west.

Hector MacLean and five clansmen lifted the coffin onto their shoulders and slowly moved it towards a finely carved tombstone. Scougall tried to make out the inscription but he was too far away. A churchman emerged from the crowd and began a prayer in Gaelic. The words seemed to merge with the wind as the coffin was lowered into the ground. The Gaelic flowed from his mouth, invoking God to look after the soul of Sir Lachlan.

Mourners came forward to pass on their condolences to the close family. Scougall lost sight of Hector MacLean and his sister in the crush around the graveside. Was Glenbeg there in the crowd? Scougall's eyes nervously darted from face to face.

Suddenly he felt a hand on his elbow.

'Davie, I must talk with you.'

MacKenzie started to lead him back towards the castle. The sound of the pibroch filled the air with a haunting elegy for the dead chief. Scougall looked back and spotted the solitary figure of Ann MacLean heading in the same direction as they were. His steps faltered.

'We have no time to lose, Davie. We must return as fast as we can to the castle.'

'But what of Sir Lachlan's funeral, sir? Surely we cannot leave. It would be ill-mannered and we have come so far.'

'All eyes are upon the graveside. We must act now.'

'But, who…?' began Scougall.

Without giving an answer, MacKenzie ran up a small hillock. Scougall followed in confusion. He had to stop beside the first tree to retch, spitting a mouthful of yellow bile onto the ground. By an effort of pure willpower he forced himself to run on, catching up with MacKenzie at the bottom of the field which led on to the causeway.

'What are we doing, sir?'

'I have no time to talk now,' panted MacKenzie. His face was bright red and he was breathing heavily. 'Come!'

Both men ran across the causeway towards the castle gates. At the far end MacKenzie stopped and leaned against the large wooden planks to catch his breath. He held his face close to the wood as if listening to the vibrations within the timber. Scougall reached the gates a few seconds later and also stood panting, the palms of his hands resting on his knees.

'What is this madness, sir?' he wheezed, now feeling slightly better; at least the run from the burial ground had cleared his head.

'I have no time for conversation, Davie!' MacKenzie stared at Scougall with an intense expression that he now recognised. There was a slight pulsing in the small bag under MacKenzie's left eye.

'Follow me, do not make any noise,' he said in a peremptory tone.

MacKenzie carefully pulled one of the gates open and they slipped into the courtyard, where the distant sound of the pipes reached them now and again with the wind. MacKenzie moved to the main entrance of the castle and opened the iron door. It made a rasping screech. They were quickly through, but stood frozen in the hallway listening for any sound from within.

They began to move down a passageway to the right. As they crept along, Scougall's attention was drawn to a line of portraits, the ancestors of Sir Lachlan peering down as if watching impostors.

MacKenzie stopped and pointed towards the stair that led to the chamber where they had examined the contents of the casket. They inched their way round the spiral and onto the first floor of the castle. With a start, Scougall saw that his master held a small dagger in his right hand. It looked ridiculously ineffectual.

They reached the door of the chamber and listened. Faint sounds reached them through the thick oak door. Scougall felt his heart pounding violently and began to sweat again as MacKenzie firmly pushed the door open and strode inside.

CHAPTER 35
A Conversation by the Fire

A TALL FIGURE dressed in a long black cloak stood at the fireplace with his back to the door. As MacKenzie and Scougall entered, he thrust a roll of paper into the flames. A wooden casket fell from his other hand and smashed into pieces on the floor. The man turned and the handsome face of Mr Primrose greeted them. Scougall was dumbfounded. He had been convinced they would find Glenbeg in the room.

'Mr Primrose, what are you doing here at such a time?' he blurted out.

'I could ask you the same question, Mr Scougall,' replied Primrose. There was no hint of his usual charm.

'Destroying the documents that we examined yesterday, Davie,' said MacKenzie, his eyes fixed on Primrose.

'But why should Mr Primrose do such a thing?' Scougall's voice was querulous with confusion.

'Because Mr Primrose has come here to eliminate the evidence that indicates his responsibility for the murder of Sir Lachlan and the apothecary Jossie.'

'I am intrigued, Mr MacKenzie, how you have come to the conclusion that I had any hand in these wretched acts. I fear that you are deluded.'

'I can assure you, sir, my faculties are in order and I am under no delusions. The conclusion I have reached is thoroughly considered and rests on hard fact. The evidence I have found, with the help of Mr Scougall, has convinced me that you were responsible for both crimes.'

Primrose stood motionless, his face giving nothing away.

'From the first I have dismissed suicide as a possibility,' MacKenzie continued. 'Some conjectured that the problems which had afflicted Sir Lachlan over many years had risen to overwhelm him, but I had known him as a friend and had acted as his legal adviser since we were both young men. He was not remotely predisposed to take his own life. I noted that the documents in his chamber in Smith's house were in a disturbed state, indicating that a hasty search had been made following his murder. The sound of an intruder probably interrupted the killer's search, for he was not, as we found out, the only one to return to John Smith's lodgings that night. Our good Mr Hope came back for matters of quite a different nature. Unwittingly he became a key witness – the cloaked figure he saw on the stairs convinced me that Sir Lachlan's death was indeed murder.'

'I see you rest your so-called case on the word of a fornicating hypocrite and manufacturer of spurious herbal remedies.'

'Hope may be a fool and an adulterer,' said MacKenzie, 'but he is not a murderer. He does not possess the ruthless nature of a killer and he had been secure in the knowledge that Sir Lachlan would keep his indiscretions secret.

'Campbell of Glenbeg was viewed by some as the most likely candidate. He was a notorious drunkard and gambler. Gruesome tales clung to him like craws around a corpse, rumours which you yourself were eager to keep in fresh circulation. But I knew that Glenbeg was very close to Sir Lachlan, practically the only man to have stood by him. What motive would he have had to kill such a benefactor? A fit of drunken debauchery was suggested, but the state of Sir Lachlan's chamber in Smith's house did not indicate that kind of attack.

'There were others present that night, but they had little motive and can easily be dismissed. Smith and his wife had hoped to marry their daughter to Hector MacLean. But was Sir Lachlan's opposition enough to drive a canny Edinburgh burgess who had accumulated capital over many years to commit murder? I do not think so.

'The chief's two men might have killed their master in a drunken plot, but again, this seemed highly unlikely. Their families depended directly on Sir Lachlan's patronage and evidence from the murder scene suggested that no irrational killing had occurred. At an early stage therefore, by a careful study of the characters, I had narrowed the field down to two men: yourself and Hector MacLean.'

'But what of Ann MacLean, sir,' Scougall interrupted. 'I was sure that I just caught sight of her leaving her father's graveside alone.'

'Davie, I will hazard a guess that she and George Scott are escaping to begin their new life together. I have observed that relations between Ann and Hector have become ice cold. Hector was as strongly against her marriage to Scott as his father had been. The lovers have reverted to the simple elopement they probably planned when Sir Lachlan was alive – a much less troublesome solution than committing double murder. I was also convinced on meeting Scott that he was a man of sound character.

'There was little at first to indicate that you, Mr Primrose, could have anything to do with the killings,' continued MacKenzie, his eyes fixed on the young advocate. 'After all you were one of Sir Lachlan's own lawyers who had acted for him over the last few years and had just secured a famous victory in the Session. However, I took it upon myself to examine the family history of all my characters. Genealogy may be a dry discipline, but there is much to commend it. The subject often provides the skeleton of history on which we can place the body of life. The story of your kin is typical of many Scottish families in this troubled century, but there were a few details which did make interesting reading, in particular the disgrace of your uncle in the 1620s and his subsequent disappearance.'

'We have heard much conjecture, Mr MacKenzie, and you obviously set great store by your so-called "instinct" but you have provided no evidence,' Primrose interrupted.

'If you will allow me, Mr Primrose. Yesterday we saw the portrait of Sir Lachlan that was painted on the afternoon before his death displayed on his coffin. I must praise the skilful artistry of Mr Henryson, for he carefully recorded all the objects on the table beside Sir Lachlan's bed on the afternoon before his murder. When I examined the table the next morning in the company of Mr Stirling we found Sir Lachlan's favourite book, a wine glass and a plain white kerchief. The painting of Henryson clearly shows these three objects, but the linen kerchief is embroidered with a small sailing galley – the coat of arms of the MacLeans of Glenshieldaig. The one I had found had no such embellishment. However, the kerchief you used to wipe your jacket at Boortree House possessed an identical motif. I believe it possible, Mr Primrose, that in your haste to leave Sir Lachlan's chambers you inadvertently picked up the wrong handkerchief. It was that same one you took from a pocket when you looked for something to mop up the wine. Not a conclusive piece of evidence, I agree, but certainly suggestive.'

Primrose looked relieved and burst into a whinnying laugh:

'Really Mr MacKenzie, you will have to do better than that. I am to be convicted on the evidence of a mad uncle and a handkerchief which Sir Lachlan gave me as a gift?'

'Oh no, sir, there is more – much more. The documents that Mr Scougall and I located in Sir Lachlan's secret casket are the key to this mystery. Thanks to a little whisky we were able to determine that the instruments were forged. This gave me the chance to test my theory. Sir Lachlan and his son had been at loggerheads for years and as anyone well versed in Highland history will be aware, enmity between a chief and his son is common. Indeed it has led to a number of documented patricides. However, one clear piece of evidence indicated that he was not the killer. When Hector was told of the existence of the casket this morning Tibbie MacLean informed me that he was anxious that the contents should be given to me to examine. He was hardly likely to do so if he was the killer and knew they contained forgeries linked to his father's murder. But while we waited in the courtyard before the coffin was carried to the burial ground, I asked Lady MacLean to inform you of the existence of the casket. I expected, if my suspicions were correct, that you would take advantage of the burial to destroy the forged instruments.' MacKenzie halted his narrative for a few moments. 'And here you are, Mr Primrose.'

'Here I am Mr MacKenzie, and behold,' Primrose smiled and pointed to the fire, 'they have been cast into the eternal flames.' He looked down into the grate where the smouldering remains could be seen. 'I must compliment you on your pertinacity, albeit in the absence of proof. Your analysis is good on many points, but not in its entirety. It feels to me that these documents were just part of a strange dream which has afflicted me over the last while and from which I am now awakening.'

'The list of creditors you provided Mr Scougall with indicated Sir Lachlan owed large sums to a very great number of people,' MacKenzie cut in sharply. 'But there was a name on the list that I did not recognise. I thought this most unusual, considering that I advised Sir Lachlan on most of his financial affairs. James Sovrack – the name has a Polish or Bohemian ring to it. I thought long and hard and got nowhere, until Mr Scougall lay on a grass verge recovering from his sail across the Forth, his head resting beside a small yellow and white flower – a primrose. The name came to me first, of course, in my own language of Gaelic – *sòbhrach*. The irony, Mr Primrose, is that your victim has fooled you from beyond the grave. When you copied the name onto the list of creditors, you made a mistake, transposing a 'k' for an 'h', the word Sovrach becoming Sovrack. Sir Lachlan wrote the word phonetically, 'bh' represented as 'v' – his written Gaelic was never good. And so, you see, he used your own name to record the illegal transactions! This was perhaps a convenience to indicate the bonds that had been raised against forged instruments, or it may have provided some kind of insurance too. We will never know.'

MacKenzie noted the first hint of agitation in the face of his quarry.

'If I may continue, Mr Primrose, I will try to describe for the benefit of my young friend what happened on the night of our soirée and why you killed the old chief. The forged documents indicate that Sir Lachlan was hoping to solve his financial problems by illegal means. The instruments created fictitious land transactions. He was thus able to issue bonds secured on land that did not exist. I believe it unlikely that your legal advice on this matter was provided free of charge. I assume you received a cut of the profits. The forgeries were no doubt made a few years back, at the start of your career, when you were trying to ingratiate yourself with the nobility. I expect you were perhaps short of a penny or two. The memory of disgrace still hung over your family.'

MacKenzie stopped for a moment and looked at Scougall. Satisfied that he was giving the narrative his undiluted attention, he turned his eyes back on Primrose.

'You worked hard at the law and in society becoming a friend of Boortree. Everything was running smoothly for you, until Sir Lachlan began to disturb the serene water of your life. I cannot be sure, but knowing his lack of financial discipline, I believe he was putting pressure on you to produce more forgeries to secure cash. By now you were a well-kent face around Parliament House, an able and proficient master of the advocate's art, a good friend of the Earl of Boortree. It was only a short while before your goal of marriage into the aristocracy would be achieved. You had no desire to risk everything by flooding the market with illegal instruments. No doubt you cautioned Sir Lachlan, advised him to bide his time. Perhaps you promised that you would be able to secure larger amounts of money for the impoverished chief when you became a son-in-law of the Earl. But as we all know, Sir Lachlan was not a patient man. He had seen how easily the documents had been drawn up and how quickly the money had appeared. He did not care that forgery was a capital offence and that many notaries have been hung on the Burgh Muir for trying to circumvent the law in this manner. He may even have threatened to reveal the existence of the forgeries. But you were not the kind of man to be overwhelmed by events – you decided to take things into your own hands. On that fateful day, you pleaded Sir Lachlan's case in the Session with all your skill. During the soirée, or before it, you arranged to meet him later in his bedchamber. After you had left with us you went to your own chambers, as you have said, but later returned to Smith's house. Sir Lachlan must have given you keys and he was waiting for you. I do not know what arguments ensued – what heated debates – but you ended with a toast. Perhaps you agreed to make further forgeries. Sir Lachlan was already drunk and it was easy to encourage him to have one more glass. It was easy to apply a few drops of poison to his glass, using your kerchief to avoid contact with the skin. Sir Lachlan drank heartily, believing his financial woes might at last be coming to an end – but within seconds he collapsed onto his bed, dragging the plaid he had worn that afternoon over himself. You made a search of his documents, hoping he had taken the forgeries with him to Edinburgh as you had requested – but he had not. Stupidly you picked up the kerchief on his table, mistaking it for your own, and put it in your pocket. Disturbed by a sound from the floor above – perhaps Mr Hope preparing to depart – there was not time to rearrange the documents and you hastily made your way out. On your way down you were seen by the minister. However, fortune was on your side, for the short-sighted Hope was unable to identify you under your cloak.'

MacKenzie again stopped briefly. Primrose did not move, presenting an inscrutable visage as if posing for his own portrait.

'The next morning, during Mr Stirling's interviews, you overheard that he had ordered his men to question the city apothecaries. It must have been a blow to discover that the Crown Officer was not treating the case as suicide as you had hoped and I think it was at this point you panicked. I must admit I am not sure of the exact train of events from here. Perhaps you can help me, Mr Primrose?'

Primrose remained silent.

'Then let me hazard a guess. You knew how meticulously the old apothecary recorded his administrations. The risk that he might have recognised you was too great. The old man came to the door, opened it and was attacked savagely. You were taking a grave risk, you might have been seen in Steel's Close.'

'Do you think I would lower myself to murder an old creature like Jossie?' Primrose said with disgust.

MacKenzie ignored his interjection.

'Darkness, however, provided the cover. You dragged him down the close, along the pathway overlooking the Nor' Loch and threw him over a steep drop. You immediately returned to the shop and removed the most recent pages from his ledger. Mr Scougall and I examined the scene on the following day and believed that we had intercepted the murderer. I now think we only disturbed an opportunistic thief who had hoped to benefit from Jossie's stock of rare medicines. The brooch we found seems to have been unconnected with the crime. You had now killed twice in the space of two days, Mr Primrose. But somehow you managed to appear your usual self at the betrothal feast of your future sister-in-law; a most accomplished piece of self control. Our London actors could learn a thing or two from you! However, words spoken by me at the party left you with an uneasy feeling. Our investigations were thorough and it was possible we were on your trail. You could not be sure – better to cover all eventualities. A deal with the caterans was easily made. Instead of travelling to Culross you made straight for Perth where you arranged for our assassination the night Mr Scougall and I met Glenbeg. You almost succeeded. Those men had their knives at our throats. We were seconds from being slain. Young Mr Scougall's vision of the Highlands was almost realised. As is often the case, the strings of discord were being pulled by a Lowlander – your good self.'

There was now contempt in MacKenzie's expression. As he reached the climax of his speech, his voice became louder and his eyes sparked with rage.

'But fate intervened, Mr Primrose, or perhaps God came to our rescue! Mr Scougall had prayed for such protection in the very church where you are soon to be installed as an elder. The MacGregors, the same clan that your uncle had spent so much time suppressing, were on the trail of the caterans – we were miraculously saved! Your priority was now to destroy the evidence and I knew you would seize the first opportunity.'

'A most entertaining story, Mr MacKenzie. But you must realise that this far-fetched tale will not stand up in a court of law.'

'We have evidence, Mr Primrose.' MacKenzie withdrew the scroll of documents from his cloak. 'Yesterday, after Mr Scougall and I examined the contents of the casket, I removed them, putting papers belonging to Mr Scougall in their place. I am sorry, Davie, but Mr Primrose has condemned your reflections on church government to the eternal flames.'

Primrose brought his fist down on the mantelpiece and sent a candlestick reeling across the floor.

'I would advise you to return those to me, Mr MacKenzie!'

Primrose pulled a pistol from his jacket, cocked the hammer, extended his arm and pointed the flintlock at the older lawyer.

Scougall cried out in panic: 'No! Stop, Primrose! No!'

CHAPTER 36
A Conclusion to this Grim Affair

'DON'T BE A damned fool, man!'

The shout came from a figure standing at the open door. Stirling had been listening to the conversation outside and now entered the room. As Primrose turned his head to see who it was, the Crown Officer's pistol went off. A haze of smoke and a strong smell of gunpowder accompanied the blast. Stirling had missed his target. A huge hole was visible in a portrait on the far wall.

MacKenzie lunged towards Primrose, partly knocking him off his feet and causing him to drop his gun. But the younger advocate was more nimble than his middle-aged opponent and thrust him back into Scougall. They both clattered into a wooden wardrobe, allowing Primrose to recover his weapon. As Stirling moved forward a second shot was fired. The Crown Officer looked down to see blood seeping through his jacket just below the elbow. His arm had been hit. He made a feeble attempt to pull Primrose down with his good arm, but was pushed aside and struck a glancing blow to the head. The young advocate fled through the doorway.

'After him!' yelled MacKenzie.

They followed Primrose into the corridor and moved as quickly as they could down the narrow staircase – one level, then two, then three – heading below ground, into the lower reaches of the castle. It was like descending the spiralled belly of a serpent. At the bottom was a cavernous room – one of the kitchens which catered for the insatiable kinsmen of Glenshieldaig. All of the cooks were at the funeral ceremony. A fire burned low in a stone fireplace, in which hung a huge iron spit. The wooden tables were covered with the leftovers from yesterday's feast. On the smoke-grimed walls were an array of hundreds of pots and pans. In the centre of the room was a large well-head descending into a deep well. The cast iron cover had been raised. Primrose stood behind it.

There were no other doorways, but to the right in a recess high on the wall was a square grain-hatch, which let in a shaft of light and lit up the barrel-vaulted ceiling.

'Good God Primrose!' shouted MacKenzie. 'Your game is up – the hangman's noose is round your neck. Surrender yourself with some dignity.'

'Am I to be taken by an old man, a snivelling boy and a cripple?' Primrose sneered.

Stirling was trying to support his arm, which was riven with agonising muscle spasms. He knelt on the floor, feeling anger rise hot inside him.

The grin on Primrose's face grew wider.

He reached inside his right breast pocket and removed a small silver pistol.

'My insurance, gentlemen. I'm afraid it is your game that is up, MacKenzie.'

As Primrose's thumb moved to cock the pistol, there was a swift movement from the shadows below the grain shaft. A figure was barely visible behind him. The grin on Primrose's face subsided. The intense stare fixed on MacKenzie did not falter, but he gave a gurgling cough, brought up a black mouthful of blood and slumped forward. His immaculately dusted periwig fell from his head onto the ground; the gun tumbled into the well. His body lay arched over the small wall enclosing the well shaft. Embedded in his back between his shoulder blades was a Highland broadsword.

'Glenbeg!' called MacKenzie.

The old Highlander moved forward to remove the sword; then, with his left hand, grabbed the back of Primrose's breeches and heaved him over the edge.

'A fitting resting place for a lawyer! And such an arrogant one, gentlemen. He promised to redeem my debts.' The Highlander nodded his head to indicate Primrose. 'Every one of them – every last one – so I would owe nothing.'

'I suspected you were implicated in some way although not the ringleader. Alistair MacGregor secured your name as the cateran's paymaster, but I was not sure about your role in the other murders,' said MacKenzie.

'I have been enslaved for forty years in a prison of bonds – chains of paper written by lawyers like you and him and finally I was to be free. I had no choice, John. It had to be.'

'Then you sold your soul to the Devil, Glenbeg. Sir Lachlan's blood is on your hands.'

'I merely provided the poison. Primrose administered it. I should have sought it elsewhere, but I went to Jossie, for I knew him well. It was too easy – I was a long-standing customer. He had often provided me with drugs and medicines to ease my pains – arsenic was mine for a small price. Sir Lachlan's death was supposed to appear to the world as suicide. Primrose should have left a note. Things did not proceed as planned. There was a trail and it had to be dealt with.'

'But what of Jossie – an innocent old man?'

'An unfortunate complication.'

'And the employment of caterans to dispatch Davie Scougall and myself?'

'A swift death by the knife is better than many – and

in your beloved Highlands! Be still, MacKenzie. I have no quarrel with you now. I have repaid my debt – your life has been saved.' Glenbeg looked up towards the grain hatch. 'And now you will let me go.'

'You know I cannot do that. The kin of Sir Lachlan demand justice as does the family of Jossie.'

For once Scougall found himself acting before he thought. Suddenly he was on his knees and under one of the long tables, just escaping a blow from Glenbeg's sword. Scuttling his way along the wall as fast as he could, he emerged at the other side of the room and grabbed a copper pan. Running straight at Glenbeg, he slammed it down on his head. The tall Campbell let out a cry and stumbled to the floor. But before Scougall could take advantage, he felt an icy grip on his ankle. A bony hand pulled with terrific force, bringing the young notary to the ground. Glenbeg heaved himself back to his feet and raised his sword.

'Gillesbuig! No!' MacKenzie yelled. Glenbeg, distracted by hearing his Gaelic name, which was rarely used by any of his acquaintances, hesitated, perhaps reminded of some incident from the distant past before his mother had been taken from him. He looked up towards the grain hatch and with a dexterity that would not have been expected in such a tall man, jumped away from Scougall and began to climb the grain sacks below the opening. Within seconds he had escaped through the hatch.

'Come, Davie! Quick!' shouted MacKenzie. 'He's in the courtyard.'

Leaving Stirling to nurse his injured arm, the two lawyers raced through the door of the kitchen, down a short passage and out into the bright light of the courtyard, just in time to see Glenbeg making for the castle gates. But the appearance of one of the handful of guards who had not attended the burial of the chief diverted him to another door at the corner of the quadrangle. He disappeared within, pursued by MacKenzie and Scougall. Glenbeg's footsteps could be heard racing up the stairs as they started to climb after him. The winding staircase seemed to go on forever – up and up, for six floors. At last they reached a door and were suddenly out into the cold morning air, on a battlement of the castle. The light was blinding as it was now almost midday. Glenbeg stood about ten paces away. His pursuers stopped, panting vigorously.

When he had caught his breath MacKenzie spoke softly, his anger dissipated.

'Glenbeg, it is over – give yourself up. There has been too much killing already – lay down your weapon.'

The old Highlander did not speak. Instead he raised his broadsword above his head and looked up at it, a hint of madness in his eyes. Then he threw it with all his might above the castle battlements. As it rose against the crystal blue and started its fall back to earth, he spoke to MacKenzie in Gaelic, in tones both fierce and pitiful: *'Fanaidh duine sona ri sith, is bheir duine dona duibh-leum.'* There was a silence, then he added, *'Fanaidh Moisean ri latha.'*

With that, Glenbeg hurled himself over the battlements.

The two lawyers looked down on the crumpled body lying far below in the courtyard of Glenshieldaig Castle, his sword gleaming close by.

'God have mercy on his soul,' Scougall murmured.

Glenbeg's green plaid enveloped him, but dark blood was visible around his head; his skull had been smashed into pieces.

In the distance, a piper was leading the mourners back to the castle from Sir Lachlan's graveside.

MacKenzie's voice was as subdued as the lament which carried to their ears on the bitter wind.

'Davie, I think the Devil has had his day.'

Historical Note

THE SEVENTEENTH CENTURY was a tumultuous period in Scottish History: famine, pestilence, revolution, war; bitter divisions between Protestant and Catholic, Episcopalian and Presbyterian, Highlander and Lowlander; alchemy, blasphemy trials and witch hunting. But it was also the century in which the modern world was born: scientific enquiry, stock market investment, political rights.

In this age of turbulence there were winners and losers. The rise of the legal profession was as relentless as their escalating fees. Many Edinburgh lawyers, especially advocates, became hugely rich.

Others fared less well. Highland chiefs were under pressure from a government which wanted to bring them into line, persuade them to resolve their disputes in court and not by feud. Having borrowed vast sums to spend on new castles, foreign luxuries and trips to Court in London, they had major financial problems. When the debt binge ended on the outbreak of civil war, many faced ruin. The years of the late seventeenth century were a grim struggle for survival.

Some chiefs saw the way the wind was blowing and sent their younger sons to be trained as lawyers in Edinburgh. These 'clan lawyers' provided cheap legal advice and represented them in the central courts. John MacKenzie was such a lawyer.

If you want to learn more about Highland chiefs in seventeenth century Scotland, the following works of history are recommended:

A.I. Macinnes. *Clanship, Commerce and the House of Stuart, 1603–1788*. East Linton: 1996.
R.A. Dodgshon. *From Chiefs to Landlords: Social and Economic Change in the Western Highlands and Islands, c.1493–1820*. Edinburgh: 1998.
P. Hopkins. *Glencoe and the End of the Highland War*. Edinburgh: 1986.

The English Spy

Donald Smith

ISBN 1 905222 82 3 PBK £8.99

He was a spy among us, but not known as such, otherwise the mob of Edinburgh would pull him to pieces.
JOHN CLERK OF PENICUIK

Union between England and Scotland hangs in the balance. Propagandist, spy and novelist-to-be Daniel Defoe is caught up in the murky essence of eighteenth-century Edinburgh – cobblestones, courtesans and kirkyards. Expecting a godly society in the capital of Presbyterianism, Defoe engages with a beautiful Jacobite agent, and uncovers a nest of vipers.

Subtly crafted... and a rattling good yarn. STEWART CONN

Delves into the City of Literature, and comes out dark side up. MARC LAMBERT

Anyone interested in the months that saw the birth of modern Britain should enjoy this book. THE SUNDAY HERALD

Excellent... a brisk narrative and a vivid sense of time and place. THE HERALD

The Fundamentals of New Caledonia

David Nicol

ISBN 0 946487 93 6 HBK £16.99

David Nicol takes one of the great 'what if?' moments of Scottish history, the disastrous Darien venture, and pulls the reader into this bungling, back-stabbing episode through the experiences of a time-travelling Edinburgh lad press-ganged into the service of the Scots Trading Company.

The time-travel element, together with a sophisticated linguistic interaction between contemporary and late 17th-century Scots, signals that this is no simple reconstruction of a historical incident.

The economic and social problems faced by the citizens of 'New Caledonia', battered by powerful international forces and plagued by conflict between public need and private greed, are still around 300 years on.
JAMES ROBERTSON, author *The Fanatic* and *Joseph Knight*

A breathtaking book, sublimely streaming with adrenalin and inventiveness...
SCOTTISH BOOK COLLECTOR

The Price of Scotland

Douglas Watt

ISBN 1 906307 09 1 PBK £8.99

The catastrophic failure of the Company of Scotland to establish a colony at Darien in Central America is one of the best known episodes in late 17th century Scottish history. The effort resulted in significant loss of life and money, and was a key issue in the negotiations that led to the Union of 1707.

What led so many Scots to invest such a vast part of the nation's wealth in one company in 1696?

Why did a relatively poor nation think it could take on the powers of the day in world trade?

What was 'The Price of Scotland'?

In this powerful and insightful study of the Company of Scotland, Douglas Watt offers a new perspective on the events that led to the creation of the United Kingdom.

Exceptionally well-written, it reads like a novel... if you're not Scottish and live here – read it. If you're Scottish read it anyway. It's a very, very good book. I-ON

Bad Catholics

James Green

ISBN 1 906817 07 3 PBK £6.99

Shortlisted for the CWA New Blood Dagger Award

It's a short step from the paths of righteousness...

Jimmy started off as a good Catholic altar boy. Growing up in Irish London meant walking between poverty and temptation, and what he learnt on the street wasn't taught by his Church. As a cop, though some called him corrupt and violent, his record was spotless and his arrest rates were high.

It's a long time since he left the Force and disappeared, and now Jimmy is trying to go straight. But his past is about to catch up with him. When one of the volunteers at the homeless shelter where he works is brutally murdered, a bent copper tips off a powerful crime lord that Jimmy is back in town. However, Jimmy has his own motives for staying put... and can he find the killer before the gangs find him?

The first in the thrilling new Jimmy Costello series.

Luath Press Limited
committed to publishing well written books worth reading

LUATH PRESS takes its name from Robert Burns, whose little collie Luath (*Gael.*, swift or nimble) tripped up Jean Armour at a wedding and gave him the chance to speak to the woman who was to be his wife and the abiding love of his life. Burns called one of 'The Twa Dogs' Luath after Cuchullin's hunting dog in Ossian's *Fingal*. Luath Press was established in 1981 in the heart of Burns country, and is now based a few steps up the road from Burns' first lodgings on Edinburgh's Royal Mile. Luath offers you distinctive writing with a hint of unexpected pleasures.

Most bookshops in the UK, the US, Canada, Australia, New Zealand and parts of Europe either carry our books in stock or can order them for you. To order direct from us, please send a £sterling cheque, postal order, international money order or your credit card details (number, address of cardholder and expiry date) to us at the address below. Please add post and packing as follows: UK – £1.00 per delivery address; overseas surface mail – £2.50 per delivery address; overseas airmail – £3.50 for the first book to each delivery address, plus £1.00 for each additional book by airmail to the same address. If your order is a gift, we will happily enclose your card or message at no extra charge.

Luath Press Limited
543/2 Castlehill
The Royal Mile
Edinburgh EH1 2ND
Scotland
Telephone: 0131 225 4326 (24 hours)
Fax: 0131 225 4324
email: sales@luath.co.uk
Website: www.luath.co.uk